THE MARRIAGE
MASQUERADE

Visit us at www.boldstrokesbooks.com

By the Author

Share the Moon

The Marriage Masquerade

THE MARRIAGE MASQUERADE

by

Toni Logan

2021

THE MARRIAGE MASQUERADE

ISBN 13: 978-1-63555-914-9

This Trade Paperback Original Is Published By
Bold Strokes Books, Inc.
P.O. Box 249
Valley Falls, NY 12185

First Edition: August 2021

CREDITS
Editor: Barbara Ann Wright
Production Design: Susan Ramundo
Cover Design By Tammy Seidick

Acknowledgments

A heartfelt thank you to Radclyffe, Sandy, and the incredible team at Bold Strokes Books. I am honored and forever grateful to be a part of this amazing family. Thank you.

A special shoutout to Barbara Ann Wright, editor extraordinaire, for her patience and guidance. I am a better writer because of you.

To my wonderful friends, thank you for always being there for me. You guys keep me smiling. I love you.

And the biggest thank you goes to you, the reader, for taking a chance on this book. I hope you enjoy reading it as much as I enjoyed writing it.

Dedication

To Jenn, Paula, Lisa, Jan, and Eddie.
Thank you for the Maui memories.

CHAPTER ONE

The sun shining through the driver's side window felt warm and welcoming on Jayden Wheaton's face. According to the news, it was twenty-one degrees out this morning, with a windchill factor that was so bitterly cold, she thought her nipples would freeze in perky status. "I hate winter," she grunted to herself as she placed a hand on the window. She felt the frosty bite of the glass and wondered yet again why she wasn't lucky enough to have been born in southern California or Florida. Someplace, anyplace, that was sunny and warm all year long.

Instead, when her birth number came up, her stork had flown to Missouri in the dead of winter, during the worst snowstorm in over a century, and at the precise moment a citywide power outage hit. An omen. She was doomed to forever live out her life in overstuffed coats and fuzzy leggings.

She eased her car into the middle of the intersection, flipped her left turn signal, and waited for the upcoming delivery truck to pass. *I should just pick my ass up and move.*

She tapped on the steering wheel to the beat of a song blaring from the radio. Her relationship with Carol had been on life support for months, and last year, her dad had uprooted to Canada to be with wife number three. What was really keeping her in a place she no longer wanted to be? *Fear.*

Jayden sighed. Fear of the unknown had always crippled her. She was a self-described risk adverse person, and she associated anything that had an unknown outcome as a risk.

As the truck made its way into the intersection, a text notification chimed on her phone. She frowned when Carol's name popped up. "What'd I do this—"

Her body whipped violently sideways, the seat belt digging into her thick winter coat as it struggled to hold her in place. Debris became airborne and flew around her as the horrific sound of metal folding around her body assaulted her ears. A searing pain shot up her left leg, and the metallic taste of blood filled her mouth. Jayden screamed as the world began to spin uncontrollably. So much spinning, so much noise, so much pain.

"Make it stop," she gurgled and choked. "Make it stop!"

She jerked awake. Her heart pounded as sweat beaded on her forehead. She blinked as she took quick rapid breaths. Unfamiliar male and female voices worked their way into her brain as the TV slowly came into focus.

"Girlfriend, you were having a sex dream, weren't you?" Jayden's best friend Andy sat next to her on the couch, smiling. He reached into the large bowl sitting between them, grabbed a handful of popcorn, and shoved it in his mouth.

"What? No," She rubbed the back of her hand across her forehead as she repositioned herself. The latest generic pain pills her doctor had prescribed were making her much drowsier than usual. She made a mental note to bring that up during her next appointment.

"Sweetheart," Andy said as he chomped, "you were moaning so loud, you put a cat in heat to shame."

She took a few deep breaths and as soon as she felt her heart rate return to normal, she turned to him. "I was dreaming about the accident."

His smirk morphed into a sympathetic frown. "Wow, you haven't had one of those in a while."

"I know." She placed her left hand on her sweats and began massaging her thigh.

"Pain kicking in?"

"Always," She shook off the visuals that were fresh in her head and grabbed a fistful of popcorn. "What'd I miss?" She nodded toward the TV, purposely changing the subject.

"Not much. My handsome hero has decided he really does want to be with said heroine, but I don't understand why. I mean, please, the woman may be beautiful, but she's a total bitch."

Jayden chuckled. "Yeah, and I know from experience that never ends well."

"My point exactly."

She rocked forward on the couch, placed her hand on the coffee table for balance, and struggled to stand. "Can I get you anything?"

"Another beer and a boyfriend."

"The beer I can deliver, but I'm pretty sure we're all out of men." She limped into the kitchen.

Andy called, "Guess we'll have to pick one up next time we go out."

She returned with a bottle in one hand and two small white pills in the other. She handed Andy the beer, and hobbled back to the couch. "Well, since that's an acquired taste, I'll leave the men picking to you."

"Coward."

She flopped back down and let the pills spill out on to the coffee table. "You know it." She said as she winked.

Jayden had met Andy in the seventh grade. She'd come to his rescue after two bullies had cornered him behind the basketball bleachers. He was small-boned, skinny, and already displayed flamboyant tendencies, so he was an easy target for spineless kids to pick on.

"Leave him alone," Jayden said as she planted her feet shoulder-width apart and dug her fists deep into her pudgy sides. She was in maximum superhero stance, and she was ready to... well, she really didn't know what she was ready to do because she hadn't thought that far in advance. But one thing was for sure, she had to look damn threatening standing there doing nothing.

"Or what?" The larger of the two boys took a few challenging steps toward her, raised his arms in a boxer stance, and dared her to bring it on.

As Jayden took in this unexpected twist in her rescue plan, she realized two things. First, she knew nothing about fist fighting, so she was sure to lose, therefore derailing her attempt at rescuing Andy. And second, since she really never had a plan to begin with, her best play would be to default to her one and only true superhero talent. The thing Jayden's mom said could stop a train in its tracks and shatter windows. She called her secret weapon a gift, but her mom had another name for it that she wasn't allowed to repeat in public.

Jayden glanced at the bully and gave him an evil smile. *"Or this,"* she answered as she tilted her head back, took a deep breath, and let out the longest high-pitched scream ever released by human lungs. The sound was so ear piercingly loud that if she weren't so tone-deaf, the opera would surely have come calling.

The hands of both bullies shot to their ears as the one yelled to the other, *"Let's get out of here."* And just like that, the power of one girl's voice dissolved an army of two.

Seconds later, three teachers came running toward the bleachers, huffing questions about what happened, was someone hurt, and what was wrong.

Jayden smiled, walked over to Andy, and looped her arm around his. *"Nothing really, just a spider, but my best friend Andy came to my rescue, so we're good."*

The teachers stood in stunned silence as they sauntered into the school hallway.

Andy doubled over with laughter "You're crazy."

"Yep, and now you're crazy by association. Let's just see if those two ever bully you again."

Andy took a couple of deep breaths, and smiled. "Seriously, thanks for doing that."

She smiled back. "You're welcome." And without thinking or asking, she reached over, grabbed his hand, and started swinging it as they skipped their way down the hall.

Jayden scooped up the pills, popped them into her mouth, and gulped them down. She let out a small burp, giggled, and pushed her body into the couch cushion.

"Thought you were going to cut back on the pills?" Andy scooted closer and leaned his head on her shoulder.

"I am. It's just that my leg has been really throbbing lately."

He nodded. "Just be careful, sweetie, those things can become addicting."

"I know," she huffed. She knew he was concerned about her. Hell, in her own way, she was too. She had heard all the reports on the perils of pain pills, but right now, she needed something to take the edge off, or she was going to be in a world of hurt later tonight.

"You going to the gym tomorrow? Maybe Taylor could help with the pain?" He munched on another handful of popcorn.

She shook her head. "Thursday. Taylor has some appointment tomorrow so she pushed our session back a day." A year ago, when she finally hit the emotional line in the sand where she was tired of feeling sorry for herself, she'd joined a gym. She wanted to lose the weight she had gained in the past five years since the accident and regain some of the strength and mobility that a physical therapist had warned her might be permanently lost.

The day Jayden limped into the gym clutching the coupon that waived her one-time membership signup fee, she got hit with the sales pitch about all the extra add-ons the gym had to offer, the personal trainer program being one of them. For an extra fifty dollars a month, she could have one-on-one sessions twice a week with a body sculpting professional. Jayden quickly did the math in her head and calculated that, yes, she could afford the additional monthly cost. A laminated paper with pictures and bios of the gym's four personal trainers was pushed in front of her. It took her all of two seconds to scan the three men and one woman. "That one," she told the salesman as she pointed to a beautiful, brown-skinned, Polynesian woman with cropped black hair, smiling at the camera while flexing her way-too-perfect biceps. The name Taylor was written in a bold red font under her photo.

"Great." The salesman nodded. "I'll put you on Taylor's roster, and she'll give you a call next week to set up your first session. You'll like her. She's a body sculpting genius."

Good, she thought as she signed the contract and handed over her credit card, because her body was in desperate need of some serious sculpting.

"You know, I'm really proud of you for sticking with it." Andy's praise brought Jayden back to the present.

She sighed. "After a year, you'd think I would have lost more weight and gained more muscle." It wasn't like she wanted to be thin or even athletic. She had always maintained what her mom called a big boned body, and she was just fine with that. She felt comfortable being curvy, but she didn't feel comfortable lugging around the extra forty pounds she'd packed on since the accident. If she could just get back to her normal weight, she would feel so much better.

"That's because these hands"—Andy wiggled his fingers—"have been gifted by the gods to create fabulous and delicious food for us mere mortals."

"Yeah, well, the sweet nectar of your talent is wreaking havoc on my once sexy body." She patted her stomach.

"Your body is still sexy, honey, and you'll get there…just give it time."

Time. Jayden snorted as she thought about the word that would always and forever define who she *was*. The time before the accident, and the time after. How could something that happened in less than sixty seconds rob her of so much?

CHAPTER TWO

Taylor Braxton followed the woman whose hips swayed in an exaggerated manner due to the restrictive fabric of the skin-tight, navy-blue skirt and equally restrictive three-inch spiked heels. The fact that they made it to the end of the corridor without the woman suffering a sprained ankle or needing chiropractic care was impressive.

They stopped outside a closed door with a bronze wall plaque that read, *Michael Jefferies, Attorney at Law*. The woman tapped three times on the thick, dark-stained wood, and turned the gold-plated knob when she heard the muffled reply. "Come in." She opened the door enough to let Taylor step around her, then promptly closed it.

"Have a seat, Taylor." Michael Jefferies extended his hand as he gestured toward one of two empty chairs that faced his oversized oak desk. He was a round, balding man, wearing a navy-blue suit and a standard white-collared shirt. His office, like his chosen dress attire, was basic and without flare. All the decorations looked like props from the set of a TV law show. Framed certificates of accomplishment were precisely spaced and hung on the walls. Pictures displaying an attractive, manicured woman and two kids were positioned perfectly around his desk, and a tall bookcase held the appropriate law books whose spines had the words *Will* and *Trust* sprinkled throughout the titles.

Taylor shrugged out of her thick winter coat and hung it on the back of the chair, then sat. "Thank you, Mr. Jefferies."

"Michael, please call me Michael. Would you like some water or coffee?"

Taylor shook her head. "No, but thank you," she replied as she crossed her legs and rubbed the sweat off her hands and onto her slate-gray tweed pants. She had been a nervous wreck from the moment her grandfather's lawyer contacted her and told her he needed to see her. Taylor's brain had spun a hundred different scenarios, none of which were good. She finally settled on the thought that her grandfather must have left behind a handful of debt that needed to be paid, and as his last surviving family member, she was now stuck with the burden of paying it off. *Shit. I'm living paycheck to paycheck as is.*

Michael opened the manilla folder in front of him and wasted no time in getting to the point. "First of all, I'm very sorry for your loss."

"Thank you," Taylor replied, emotionless. She was neither saddened or upset by her loss. Her grandfather had been an ass in every sense of the word. Loss was not the noun she would use to describe what she was feeling. It was more like indifference.

"As I explained over the phone, I'm handling Frank's, um, your grandfather's will, and I need to inform you of a few things regarding his personal belongings."

"Okay," she barely squeaked out the word as she closed her eyes and waited for the bad news to drop.

"Your grandfather had a substantial portfolio, consisting of shares in a variety of stocks, several IRA's, a savings and checking account, a two-bedroom condo, and a handful of personal possessions. All were to go to your mother, but upon her passing, he had me amend the will and divert all his assets to you."

Taylor opened her eyes. "He willed everything to me?"

"Yes." Michael guided over a piece of paper that had an inventory of itemized items.

She slowly picked it up and began scanning the list. "I don't understand."

"That is a list of all Frank's assets. They're now yours."

"These are all mine?"

He nodded. "Yes, they will be distributed to you to do with as you wish."

She glanced up from the paper and frowned. "So, um, now that these are all mine, how much debt am I responsible for? There's a lot on this list to pay off." She pointed to item number three. "Like grandpa's minivan."

He chuckled. "You don't understand. Everything Frank owned was paid for in full. You owe nothing. Every single one of those assets is free and clear." He sat back in his chair and let that last bit of information sink in.

"You're telling me that I don't owe anything? On any of these?"

He nodded. "Not one penny."

Taylor let out a long breath as relief and confusion spread over her body. Something wasn't adding up. "Are you sure I don't owe *anything*?"

"I'm positive." Michael leaned forward in his chair and tapped his fingers on another piece of paper in the folder. "There's, um, there's one more asset that you need to know about."

"Besides all this stuff?"

"Yes." He stopped drumming his fingers, picked up a piece of paper, and flicked it toward her. The paper floated in her direction and landed a few inches from the other. "Your grandfather owned a half-acre piece of property in Maui, with a two-story house that is presently registered with the state as a bed and breakfast."

Taylor looked up. "Maui? As in—"

"Hawaii."

She blinked. Did she just hear him right? Maui, Hawaii? Her grandfather? "I, um, I don't understand. My grandfather never had property in Maui. The only property he owned was his condo in Indiana. It overlooks a lake that he and some friends went fishing on all the time." She threw out the useless information as Michael nodded. "I never even heard him talk about Hawaii, I mean, outside of military references from the time he was stationed there. Is this a joke?"

He shook his head. "I can assure you, it is not a joke."

"But, where did he get all this money? From what I knew of Grandpa, he could barely make ends meet. At least, that's what he constantly told us."

Michael frowned as he rubbed his chin. "I don't know where Frank acquired his wealth, nor can I speak on behalf of his motives, but I can assure you, he could most definitely make ends meet. Your grandfather wasn't rich by today's standards, but he was in no way struggling. In fact, far from it."

Her stomach began to churn, and a wave of dizziness and nausea hit her. She placed her head between her knees and took a couple of deep breaths.

"Taylor? You okay? Can I get you anything?"

She held up a finger as she gestured to give her a minute. "You're telling me"—she huffed as she raised her upper body— "that my grandfather had a place in Maui for what, the past few years?"

Michael glanced at the paperwork. "Decades is a more accurate timeframe."

Taylor jumped to her feet as a surge of anger coursed through her veins. *That bastard had money and a house in Maui?* She thought about all the times she and her mom went without anything extra because they were so poor. *And he never once lent a helping hand. Not once.* She pressed her fingers against her temples as she thought about everything she and her mother had gone through.

The day after Taylor's mom had graduated from high school, she'd run away with a boy who'd lived one town over. Frank had called the police the moment he'd noticed she was gone and three days later, the cops had located the two of them hiding out in an abandoned barn. Taylor's mom had been grounded until she turned eighteen and was banned from seeing the boy again. But five months later, when she could no longer hide the baby bump, Taylor's mom had tearfully announced she was pregnant. Frank had responded by throwing her out of the house. When she'd gone in search of her teenage lover, she'd discovered his family had moved to somewhere in Arizona, or was it California? The neighbor she'd spoken to wasn't sure which.

Hungry, scared, and tired of spending days on the streets, Taylor's mom had made her way back to their neighborhood church. The secretary who'd worked in the office then called a friend of hers who ran a home for runaway teens. Fortunately for Taylor's mom, they'd had space. She'd stayed for a year, and in that time, she'd given birth to Taylor, had found a job at a local daycare, and had saved enough money to rent a small apartment.

When Taylor graduated high school, her mom had presented her with a bank account number. It was the first Taylor had ever known about the college fund her mom had started for her when she was a toddler. Every penny her mom had earned working overtime went into that account. It wasn't much, but it would be enough to get her through two years of community college. "Don't work your life away like me," her mom had said, "get a college degree and go be something special."

It was the best gift Taylor had ever received, but at the end of Taylor's first semester, her mom was diagnosed with metastatic breast cancer. Four months later, she was gone, leaving Taylor completely alone, with nothing in the bank but her college fund, which she'd quickly depleted to cover the cost of the funeral.

When she'd notified her grandfather of her mom's passing, he'd told her he would be there for the funeral and service but not before. Long after the graveside ceremony was over and everyone had left, Taylor had continued to stand with tear-soaked eyes over her mother's casket. A weathered hand on her shoulder followed by a voice that announced it was just the two of them now, had made her turn and sob into her grandfather's arms. But whatever hopes Taylor had of finally developing a relationship with Frank never materialized. He'd left the following day, and although they'd called each other from time to time, Frank had made no real attempt to be in her life. And he'd definitely made no attempt to ease Taylor's financial burdens. Even after she'd shared the news with him that she'd had to drop out of college and get two jobs to cover all the expenses, Frank had never offered a dime.

He knew I was struggling, and that I needed help, and not once did he even offer. That son of a bitch, and this whole time he's had property in Maui. Damn him.

Taylor snapped out of her trance, glanced over, and frowned. "Sorry."

With a wave of his hand, Michael gestured like it was no big deal. "The property is in the town of Kihei, off Maui's southwest shore, and from what your grandfather once told me, it's quite a nice piece of land. He said investors have been banging on his door for years, trying to get him to sell so they could turn the land into commercial property, but he refused. I think his exact quote was, 'I told them all to go to hell.'" Michael chuckled. "He told me he was one of the last holdouts in that area."

"Yep, that sounds like my grandfather," Taylor snapped as her brain continued to process the information. What was he doing with property on Maui? And more importantly, why didn't she or her mom ever know about it?

"The property has been willed to you Taylor, but there's a stipulation."

"What?"

Michael read from a small, handwritten piece of paper that he'd unclipped from the folder. "Taylor Braxton, my granddaughter and sole surviving heir, may take possession of the keys to the Maui property when, and only when, she gets married."

"Married?" The punch to her gut was immediate. Tying the knot had never been on her to-do list. In fact, just the opposite. It represented a flawed institution that more times than not, ended in divorce, anger, and heartache. No thanks. And for her grandfather to even suggest, much less force such a stipulation on her was just another reminder he never saw her for who she was. She swallowed the bitter taste of hurt that was making its way up her throat as she blinked back a tear. Even in his death, she could still feel the slap of his hurtful hand.

Michael held up his hand. "And, she must live with and remain in the committed marriage for one year. Once she has fulfilled this request, on the day after her one-year anniversary, she will be granted the deed to the property." He clipped the paper back onto the manilla folder.

Taylor felt the anger return. That goddamn son of a bitch. He knew she was gay. Hell, that was why they hadn't spoken in all these years. He wouldn't let up on his homophobic rants about her *depraved lifestyle* and how she just needed to find the right guy.

She had finally told him that if he couldn't accept her lifestyle, then they had nothing more to say to each other. The click of the phone as he hung up on her was the last sound she'd ever heard from him. And now, from his grave, he was trying to get the last laugh. *Well, screw him.* She would liquidate the other assets, pay off her debts, and be done with him forever.

Taylor stood and lifted her coat off the chair. "Well," she grunted. "That's not going to happen."

Michael nodded. "It is a bit of an odd request."

"Does it say what will happen to the property if I refuse?"

"Yes, the property will be sold, and the proceeds will go to a designated veteran's charity."

"I see." Of course they would. That was all her grandfather ever talked or cared about. He'd enlisted in the Navy after WWII, and he'd yammered on about his military buddies with more love and emotion than he'd ever expressed for Taylor or her mom. "Well." She extended her arm. "Thank you for your time, Michael, but I decline my grandfather's offer on the Maui property."

He nodded as he shook her hand. "I understand."

"Do I still get to keep the other stuff?"

"Yes, of course, only the Maui property has the stipulation."

Of course it does. It's the most valuable and most appealing.

"Maybe you would like to take some time to think about it?" He walked her to the door.

"I don't need any more time or any more manipulation from my grandfather. I will not be accepting those terms."

"Very well, then," Michael mumbled. "I'll draw up the paperwork on the other items and send it to you for review and signature."

"Thank you." Taylor placed her hand on the doorknob and froze as a thought jolted through her. "Michael?"

"Hum?"

"Does the will say that I have to be married to a man? Or does it say that I just have to be married?"

He walked over to his desk, flipped open the folder, and quickly scanned the note. "It appears that there is no language that specifies a man. Just that you must be married upon receipt of the keys. Frank's amendment was filed before same-sex marriage became legal, if that's what you're getting at."

Two can play at this game, old man. "Let's just say, hypothetically, if I were to marry a woman, it would still constitute a fulfillment of my grandfather's wishes, correct?" She briefly thought about asking a trusted male friend to join her in a fake marriage but quickly dismissed the thought. Marrying a woman under Frank's own stipulation was the poetic justice he deserved.

He slowly nodded. "That would be correct, but I don't think that's what he had in mind."

"I don't care what he had in mind. Would it fulfill the legal requirement of the stipulation?"

"Yes, yes it would."

Taylor smiled. *I'll get you yet, you bastard.* "Then hold that thought, Michael. I think I'll be coming for those keys after all. I hear wedding bells in my immediate future."

He smiled. "As you wish."

Taylor thanked him again for his time, then strolled out of the office and back toward the elevator with a renewed spring in her step. She was going to have the last laugh in her grandfather's sick marriage scheme. *What kind of man does that to his granddaughter?* She'd often wondered what had happened in Frank's life to turn him into such an asshole. Oh well, not her concern anymore. What she needed to concentrate on now was finding a woman she could trust who would agree to marry and live with her for a year and then divorce with no strings attached or emotional or financial expectations. Taylor frowned as she pressed the button to summon the elevator. She knew a grand total of zero women who fit that bill. *Hmm, this could be more complicated than I thought.*

CHAPTER THREE

I thought we'd start on the treadmill this morning if you're good with that?" Taylor said as she grabbed a clipboard.

"Yeah, that'll be fine." Jayden said as she unwrapped the knitted scarf that covered her nose and mouth and let the warmth of the gym thaw her skin. The smell of sweat and the clanging sound of weights that used to intimidate her when she walked through the doors, now set her at ease. The wall-to-wall mirrors, on the other hand, still made her feel like a foreigner in this land of sculpted bodies. Why was perfection so hard to achieve? And most importantly, why wasn't there a pill for it? Jayden smiled as she glanced at Taylor. "I'll just go put my coat and purse in the locker room and see you over there."

She caught Taylor's nod in the mirror as she hobbled past her to the locker room. *Taylor.* The woman was strikingly gorgeous in all the ways society seemed to cherish and celebrate beauty. Her eyes shifted back to her own profile in the mirror, and she paused a moment to pat her stomach. She wondered if she would ever lose the extra weight and if not, would Taylor look at her like a failure? She shifted her vision back to Taylor. She could see her watching her, so she sucked in her stomach. God, that woman gave her the feels. If only women like *that* went for women like her. Impossible. Jayden snorted as she let her stomach return to its resting shape. She didn't have the physique that she thought gym goddesses like Taylor were attracted to. *You're not in her league. Not even close.*

"Jayden." Taylor called as she continued toward the locker room. "Your limp seems a little more pronounced than usual. You doing okay?"

Jayden tripped on a blue five-pound dumbbell sitting on the floor by a bench as she turned. "Yeah." She rolled her eyes, embarrassed for being such a klutz. Seemed the only thing Taylor noticed about her body was the one thing she hated the most. "Stupid limp," she grumbled, then nonchalantly patted her thigh. "The cold always affects it. I'll be fine."

"Maybe we'll go easy on the treadmill and make up for it on the weights," Taylor said.

"Sounds good." Jayden turned back around and kicked the dumbbell, trying unsuccessfully to move it out of the way as a searing pain shot up her toe. "Great." She limped on her heel as she headed to the locker room. "Just great."

Ten minutes later, as she approached the cardio section of the gym, her breath caught as she glanced at Taylor. With her perfectly sculpted body; blue, full-length yoga tights; and a super tight, V-neck T-shirt with the gym's logo splashed across her chest, Taylor looked like she just stepped out of a Nike ad. *God.* Jayden sighed. *To have a body that actually bulges from muscles instead of donuts.*

She grabbed at the waistband of her bulky heather gray sweatpants, hiked them up, then tugged down on her equally bulky sweatshirt. She shuffled around Taylor to the back of the treadmill. She had fifty minutes to enjoy her undivided attention. She grabbed the two balance rails and, using her good leg, hopped on the machine. "I'm all yours."

"How about we start out slow, and see how your leg feels?"

"I don't know why it locks up so much in the cold weather." Jayden sighed. "I really need to move to a warmer climate."

"Yeah," Taylor said as she pushed the red button to start on a slow walking pace. "This winter has really been a bitch so far. How's that pace?"

"Good."

"Great, let's do a ten-minute warmup here, and then we'll go over to the chest press."

Jayden took her hands off the side rails and cupped her breast. "Oh good, cause these girls need to be pressed into shape."

❖

Taylor laughed as she glanced at Jayden. She had really come far in the past year since they'd started working together. Not so much physically, but mentally, she had seen huge gains in Jayden. She was no longer the beaten-down person who would go an entire session with her head down, barely talking and apologizing endlessly for not being able to successfully lift a weight or complete an exercise.

In those first few weeks, Taylor had pegged her as one of the many who would quickly drop out of the personal training program and eventually stop going to the gym all together. But by the end of the first month, she had started to see something in Jayden that reminded her of herself. It was desire. A deep-down need to change her life. So Taylor made sure to take the time to praise Jayden's gains, no matter how small. She'd become an expert at reading her physical signs and never pushed her beyond her limits.

To Taylor's delight, Jayden had not only stuck it out, but by the time she'd hit her sixth month mark, she seemed a completely different person. She was no longer quiet and self-loathing. Instead, she was talkative and upbeat. She smiled from the moment she walked into the gym until the moment she left. In ways, those gains mattered way more than muscles. She just hoped Jayden saw herself as she saw her. She was beautiful in all the ways that mattered and Taylor caught herself more than once using the mirrors to stare at her.

❖

"Everything go well at your appointment?" Jayden huffed as Taylor increased the incline to level three. "With the lawyer yesterday?"

Taylor nodded. "Yep, all's good. Looks like I'm going to get married soon."

Jayden stumbled. Taylor never so much as mentioned a girlfriend, and now she was getting married? Every fantasy she had ever had about Taylor instantly crashed down on her like a ten-ton weight. She knew she had zero chance of ever being with her, but damn it, as long as Taylor was single, she could keep the fantasies alive. But married?

Taylor jumped on the machine and straddled the rotating belt as she pressed her body firmly against Jayden's. "You okay?" she said in a soft voice as she wrapped an arm around Jayden's waist to steady her as she powered down the machine.

A jolt of electricity shot through Jayden's body. She exhaled a shaky breath as she tried to calm her libido. Even though she was well aware of her—and everyone else's crush on Taylor—she always kept it in check because deep down, she considered her a friend. Not the kind of friend she texted and talked to several times a week, more the casual, *see you around*, kind of friend. And she wasn't about to let a silly old crush get in the way of a friendship. "Yeah, no, I'm good," She replied. "Just, you know, the leg."

Married. She silently repeated the word that felt like a slap of cold water. "So." Jayden took a breath as she stood on the rubber belt, praying to the Lesbian God of Lust that Taylor would remain holding her for the remainder of their session. "Who's the lucky woman?"

"Don't know yet." Taylor jumped off the treadmill and leaned against the machine.

"Okay, back up," she said as her body shivered from the residual excitement of having Taylor's arms around her. "Are you seriously telling me you don't know who you're marrying?"

"I'm seriously telling you I don't know who I'm marrying."

"I don't understand," Jayden inquired.

"It has to do with my grandfather's will and a little business arrangement I'll need to make with someone that'll include both a marriage and a divorce."

"Okay, wait…you're going to marry someone knowing up front that you're going to divorce them?" *Okay, first of all, does this mean my fantasies are back in play? And secondly, and most important, why in the world would Taylor go through the trouble of marrying someone she has no intention of staying with?* It wasn't that Jayden ever thought of herself as being traditional, but she questioned whether or not she could ever do something like that for the sake of a business arrangement.

"Yep." Taylor spent the rest of their training session filling Jayden in. "Even in the end, my grandfather was a total asshole." Taylor sighed as they strolled into a back room full of punching bags and other miscellaneous boxing equipment. "Well, the joke's on him because as soon as I find someone I can trust, who will agree to marry me for a year, then divorce as soon as I get the deed, I'll have the last laugh." She handed Jayden the battle ropes. "One minute of slaps, ready and go."

Jayden gripped the taped off ends of each rope and moved her arms up and down, slapping them against the floor. A twinge of envy shot through her as she thought about Taylor's situation. How amazing would it be to inherit a B and B on Maui? The beaches, the ocean, the sunshine. Her movement slowed, and the slapping sound of the ropes became more like a pat as her focus drifted to palm trees and warmth. She had never been to Hawaii, but it was on her bucket list. What she would give to spend a year in paradise, soaking up the sun and…

"And…stop," Taylor's words pulled her back to reality. "Good job, Jayden, how do you feel?"

"I'll…go." Jayden gasped between heavy breaths as she dropped the ropes, put her hands on her hips, and bent over.

"What?"

"I'll go…to…Maui with you." Both her leg and her body had had enough of freezing temperatures, and this was just the catalyst she needed to get her out of the rut that had become her life. The fact that she would have to marry and divorce was the only part of the equation that wasn't appealing. She had always dreamed that her wedding would resemble a romantic picture book, and the marriage would end in a happily ever after. Not come with divorce papers already in place. Oh well. Jayden shrugged. At least she would be helping Taylor out and, in the end, both would get what they wanted. This marriage, like so many other situations that she found herself in, was just one more thing to fake her way through.

Just like she had faked her feelings of support when her dad asked how she was handling his third marriage. Or the orgasms she sometimes faked with Carol because the loveless relationship made her too numb to feel. And of course, faking a life of normalcy after the accident when deep down she was in so much physical pain and depression she thought of ending it all. Yeah, she was becoming a pro at faking her way through life.

"You, uh, you would?" Taylor stumbled.

"Well, yeah, I mean…I think it would be great for my leg to be in warmer weather, and as you know…I don't have a job or anything holding me here." After the accident, she had lawyered up, and because the trucking company's driver was ticketed at the scene for being at fault, they were anxious to settle the claim. In the end, she had received enough money to get by for the rest of her life if she maintained a somewhat minimalist lifestyle. Having been a minimum wage cashier at a mega hardware store for the past twelve years, she was a pro at stretching a dollar, so living off the settlement would be a piece of cake. The money would make her self-sufficient and would gift her the one thing she'd never thought she would have. Financial freedom. And for that, she was grateful.

She glanced at Taylor, who stood staring at her like a deer in headlights. A wave of embarrassment shot through her. Uh-oh. What if Taylor thought she wasn't even good enough to fake marry and divorce? "What?"

❖

Taylor remained silent for an awkward moment as she thought about the offer. Jayden's name hadn't popped up when she'd run through her short list of friends. She and Jayden really weren't *good* friends, but they were *good enough* friends. She took a few steps back as she sized Jayden up. She was nice, kind-hearted, had a wicked sense of humor, and was pretty easygoing. She didn't seem to have a lot of drama in her life, and from past conversations, she enjoyed her solitude as much as Taylor did. Their personalities seemed to mesh well together, and conversations between them were never strained. *Why not?*

It would only be for a year, and besides, it was becoming clear to Taylor that finding someone to marry her, quit their job for a year, and move to Maui was going to be a lot harder than she originally thought. "We'd need to sign an agreement that says we're going into this marriage as a business arrangement, and after I get the deed, we divorce. I hope that doesn't sound cold or anything, but I just thought, you know, we'll need to have it all written down since we'll be dealing with legal documents and all. Are you okay with that?"

"Yeah, of course, that would be fine." Jayden nodded. "So are you saying you're good with me doing this with you?"

"Are you good?"

"Yeah, I am. I think I'm overdue for a change of scenery."

"Then what are you doing Friday afternoon?"

"This Friday? Really?" Jayden squealed as she rapidly clapped her hands.

She's so damn cute. Taylor had a sudden urge to scoop Jayden up in her arms and hug her. But they were still trainer and client, and she didn't feel it was appropriate to cross that line. Hmm. She frowned as it dawned on her that they were about to trade one business arrangement for another. That line might become harder and harder to maintain.

"Yeah, this Friday." Taylor nodded. Why put it off? The sooner they married, the sooner she could get the deed. Payback to a grandfather who seemed to hold as many secrets as he did grudges.

❖

"Well then, I, um, I guess I'm getting married." The moment she said the word, Jayden's knees buckled. If she thought the battle ropes made her body feel weak, it was nothing compared to what she was feeling right now. *Married.* The word tickled up her and made her shiver, and although her mind knew it was nothing more than a business arrangement, her body was sure enjoying dismissing that piece of reality.

By the time she left the gym, she had fired off a dozen text messages to Andy. Tonight, fake marriage or not, they were going to celebrate.

"I got your text messages, so what's the big news you couldn't wait to tell me until I got home from work? You know I'm one of those people who has to open a present the moment I see it. That whole delayed gratification crap was created by a psychopath," Andy rambled as he shrugged out of his coat and hung it on the rack by the door.

"I know, and I'm so sorry for torturing you." Jayden grabbed his hand and led him to the kitchen. Two glasses of red wine sat by ceramic plates. Candles were lit, a small bouquet of flowers graced the middle of the table, and her best silverware was properly placed on top of cloth napkins. An extra-large pizza box sat off to the side. "I made dinner tonight." She beamed. "Well Pizza Pete's made dinner, and someone else made the wine, but I put it all together." Her culinary skills sucked, and she and Andy both knew it. But she could still set a table like there was no tomorrow, and right now, she hoped the love she put into the setting more than made up for what she lacked in the kitchen.

Andy cocked his head. "So the big news is that you figured out which wine to pair with pizza?" He opened the pizza box and squealed. "You ordered my favorite." He pulled out a cheesy piece, piled high with black olives and onions, onto his plate.

Jayden handed him a glass as she lifted hers. "First, a toast to—"

"Sweetie, you can't drink alcohol because of your meds," he interrupted.

"I know, but tonight is a special occasion, and I'll only have a sip."

"And I get to finish what you don't drink?"

"Of course." Jayden smiled. "Now, as I was saying, a toast... to the bride-to-be."

She clinked his glass, and he took a big gulp. "Oh yeah? Who's getting married?"

"I am."

Jayden had to smack him on the back three time before he was able to catch his breath. "Sorry, Andy, I guess I should have timed the big reveal a little better."

"Is this a joke?" He sat and thumped his chest with his fist as he coughed one last time.

"It's no joke, and I would be honored if you were my man of honor."

"Okay, first of all I never turn down an opportunity to glam it up, and second of all, you owe me a story worthy of an Oscar."

He picked up the slice of pizza and shoved half of it into his mouth. "I'm waiting," he mumbled as he chewed.

"Well, you know Taylor, from the gym..." She spent the next half hour filling him in and by the time she finished her story, she was wiping tears from her eyes. She still couldn't believe she'd blurted out that she would marry Taylor, much less have Taylor accept. For the next year, she was going to live with a beautiful woman on a beautiful tropical island. Fairytales like this just didn't happen to her.

"So? What do you think?" She reached over and grabbed the last slice of pizza from the box.

He leaned back in his chair. "I have a few questions. First, what are you going to do with the house?"

Jayden had put a chunk of her settlement money down on a cute three-bedroom house. Two years ago, Andy had moved in after his boyfriend had dumped him for a male model and had told him he had twenty-four hours to pack his stuff and get out. What was supposed to be temporary had turned out to be a beneficial arrangement for them both. They'd cried on each other's shoulders, ranted about their exes, and lifted the other up when they were feeling down. But more than anything else, having Andy in the house helped chase away the loneliness that had become an unwelcome but constant companion.

"Nothing. I'll be back in a year, so it won't change a thing." Jayden said.

"Good answer. Second, what's the color scheme of the wedding?"

Jayden paused. Taylor hadn't said, and she hadn't asked. Should she text her and run it by her? A voice inside her said, no, don't go there. This wedding wasn't about the color schemes or any of the fun little details that most couples discussed and agreed upon. It was a business arrangement, plain and simple. "We, um, didn't really talk about that. But as you know, my favorite color is blue."

"Tell me it's blue with a slight peach accent, and you'll win this round of questioning."

"Blue with peach, you got it." Jayden said as she visualized Taylor standing next to her wearing a dark blue tux. She knew from seeing Taylor in skintight workout clothes that she would be stunning in a tux. Her body tingled with the thought. *Oh, get a grip.* She scolded herself with the reminder that none if this was real. Not even close.

"Excellent, and third, will there be sex?"

"Andy!" She playfully backslapped his shoulder, but who was she kidding? She had thought that same thing a least a dozen times on her drive home from the gym.

"Oh, come on, a year on Maui? Please. Fake marriage or not, that place is fucking romantic."

"It's not like that. We're just friends." But Jayden had wondered how she was going to handle being with the most gorgeous woman she knew in a tropical paradise for a year and not want to be with her. *I'm going to handle it the same way I've handled my feelings for every other woman I've met since Carol. I'm going to overthink it, convince myself I'm not good enough, and do nothing.*

"Blah, blah, blah." He tapped his fingers on his thumb as he mimicked a talking mouth. "Friends to lovers…it happens all the time."

"Well, not this time. This is about Taylor fulfilling a stipulation in her grandfather's will and me getting to spend a year in Maui for free. After that, we'll divorce, and I'll come back here and get on with my life, and she'll stay there and get on with hers."

"Oh God, that sounds so depressing. I mean, think about it, you're not even married yet, and already you're planning your divorce."

"Yeah, I guess when you put it like that, it does sound kinda depressing." And pathetic. Oh well, welcome to her life.

"Can your amazingly handsome best friend come visit?"

"I'll make it a deal breaker if you can't."

He jumped up and hugged her. "I'm so happy for you."

"Well, it's not a real marriage, but maybe this will be a nice warm-up if ever I do find someone who wants to be with me." A somber cloud settled around her. Ever since her accident, she had been so self-conscious of her scar and limp that she'd allowed both to chip away at her self-esteem.

Andy sat back down. "Hey, none of that, you hear me? You'll find your happily ever after because you're an amazing and beautiful woman."

"No, Andy, I'm not…at least not anymore."

"Honey, I don't ever want to make light of what happened to you or your struggles, but the accident shattered your leg, not your libido. You're a beautiful person, Jayden. Any woman would be honored to be with you. Plus, you're my best friend, so you bring extra bonus points to the table for that."

She smiled but didn't bother to reply. She had listened to the spiel so many times. Between her therapist, Andy, and her other friends, she heard every inspiring quote ever written. And while what they said held merit, she knew she would never stop comparing her life before the accident to the one she was now living. Feeling beautiful came from the inside out, and living in a body she had grown to hate felt anything but beautiful.

Andy poured the rest of Jayden's glass into his, stood, and held out his hand. "Come on. Let's go watch a rom-com and cry over a sappy and unrealistic story. Or if you'd rather, we can troll your ex on social media and make snarky and trashy comments about her."

Jayden smiled. "Oh, that is always fun, but I think I'm in more of a rom-com mood tonight."

"Movie night it is. Then tomorrow, I'm taking you shopping."

She grabbed Andy's hand, and he helped lift her out of her chair. She stumbled a bit as she put pressure on her left leg but quickly regained her footing. "That's okay. You know how much I hate—"

"The wedding might not be real," he interrupted, "but damn it, you're going to look fucking amazing faking it."

❖

"I got your text, so what's the big news that you couldn't tell me over the phone?" Annie huffed as she slid into the opposite seat of the booth. "And please tell me there's alcohol in that amazingly exotic-looking blue drink."

"There's alcohol in this amazingly exotic-looking blue drink," Taylor said as she pushed her drink over to Annie. They'd been thick as thieves ever since kindergarten when the other kids had called her a freak for the large purple birthmark that covered most of her left cheek. Taylor had thought Annie's birthmark resembled a dog, and as such, made her all the more special.

Annie took a gulp. "Holy fuck, that's good. I'm commandeering the rest of this drink."

Taylor laughed. "I kinda figured you would." They were not sisters by blood, but they were definitely sisters in heart, and she couldn't imagine her life without Annie.

"Okay." Annie took another gulp. "Now that I'm partially liquored up, what's the big reveal?"

"I found someone to marry." Taylor smiled as she said the word, which surprised her. Since marriage had never been on her things-to-do list, she dismissed her touch of giddiness as having more to do with payback to her grandfather than marrying Jayden.

"Well, hallelujah for that. It would have killed me if you had to give up on that B and B because I'm already planning on coming out and staying for a while. So who is she, and how do you know her?"

"It's Jayden, one of my clients from the gym." She smiled again, but this time, she couldn't justify away the feelings associated with it. *Don't go there.* Jayden was doing her a favor. If she didn't stick to the arrangements, things would get complicated. Don't mess this up, she scolded herself. Besides, she knew all too well what her pattern was, and she was not about to inflict that on Jayden.

"The tall and sexy as hell woman who's training for a triathlon?"

"Nope."

"Oh, wait, I know." Annie snaped her fingers. "It's the author chick who asked you out for coffee last week."

"Still no."

"Hmm." Annie shrugged as she waved the server over. "Okay, I give, who's your bride-to-be?" The server appeared at their table. "We'll have two more of these please." Annie motioned to the empty glass that sat in front of her that had a tiny amount of blue liquid pooled at the bottom. "Now then, tell me who's going to be Mrs. Taylor Braxton for the next year."

"Remember me talking about this woman who had a bad limp from a car accident and wanted to lose some weight and regain some muscle? Baby Blue?" Taylor threw out the nickname she'd given Jayden in reference to the prettiest baby blue eyes she had ever seen. Eyes that melted her from the moment she saw them.

Annie widened her eyes. "You're marrying Baby Blue? How'd that happen?"

The server came over and placed two glasses, with turquoise liquid, umbrellas, and a slice of pineapple in front of them.

"Thanks." Taylor smiled at the woman, then returned to Annie. "Well, I was telling her about the will today during our session, and after she finished with the battle ropes, she just blurted out that she would do it."

"God, those things kick my ass."

"I know, they kick everyone's ass, but they work. Anyway, she lives off the insurance money from the accident, so she doesn't have anything holding her—"

"I still feel bad that I can't marry you," Annie interrupted, "but there's no way with mom right now that I can take the time—"

Taylor held up her hand. Annie was the first person she asked to go with her to Maui. Her and her mom were family to Taylor, and the thought of being so far away from them was painful. They'd stepped in after her mom had died and had been by her side ever since. They were the one constant in her life that she could depend on, and it would have been nice to have had them by her side on this new adventure. "Annie, don't even worry about it. It's a big ask of anyone. It just so happens that Jayden is in a position where she can do it. Besides, she thinks the warm weather will do her leg some good, and I think so too."

Annie leaned back. "You know, it's kinda poetic that you'll have the last laugh when it comes to your grandpa. He was such an ass to you. Especially after you were robbed." She took a gulp of her drink. "I almost wish he was still around just so I could see the expression on his face when you marry Jayden."

Taylor flashed back to the night she was mugged. It was four years after her mom had died. Her car was in the shop, and she was pulling extra shifts to get enough money to cover the bill. On that particular night, she had been walking home from an exhausting but profitable day waiting tables. She had made enough cash from tips alone to cover the last of the auto repairs. No more walking, she'd thought as relief washed over her. She had been so drained those past few weeks, she didn't think she could sustain the pace much longer without totally crashing.

As she headed down the street that led to her apartment complex, a man dressed in dark clothes had stepped out of nowhere and had demanded she hand over her money. Fear had shot through her body like nothing she had ever known. Her hands had instinctively tightened around her purse as she'd froze. In two quick steps, he'd reached out a muscular hand, grabbed her shirt collar, and pulled her close. She could smell the stench of alcohol permeating his breath as he'd told her one more time to hand over her money. Adrenaline and defiance had surged through her, and she had begun beating at his hand as she struggled in his grip, but his strength had far outmatched hers. She'd twisted and kicked, but she had been weak and unskilled in the art of self-defense. With his other hand, he'd begun pulling the purse off her shoulder.

"No," she'd called out as she desperately grabbed at the straps. A quick tug-of-war had ended when she was thrown to the ground like a discarded ragdoll. She'd landed facedown on the sidewalk. The sound of his footsteps retreating had echoed in her head as she'd used the last ounce of strength to twist her upper body off the sidewalk. She'd sat for a moment, trying to process everything that had just happened as tears dripped down her face.

She'd eventually staggered to Annie's apartment, and she and her mom had taken Taylor to the hospital. Her face had been scraped up, and she was going to have bruising, but fortunately, nothing had been broken. Before leaving, she had been questioned by a police officer. No, she hadn't gotten a good look at the mugger's face, and no, she didn't remember anything about him, other than he had dark clothes. The officer had nodded and told her there probably wasn't much they could do, but they would be in touch if anything came up.

Annie's mom had notified her grandfather of the mugging. Frank, in turn, had told her he was not in a position to come see her anytime soon, and that she should probably stay with Annie.

Frank had eventually showed up unannounced three weeks later and had taken Taylor out to lunch. Although the scrapes and bruises were almost healed, the impact of the mugging was becoming apparent. Nightmares haunted her sleep, and she had become jumpy and tense. And as she'd sat across from Frank that afternoon, she had started to cry. She'd wanted to melt into his arms and have him tell her that everything was going to be okay. That she was going to be okay. But instead, he'd lectured her on how she brought this on herself because she should have never been walking alone late at night. What had she been thinking? When she'd told him about her broken down car, he'd scoffed at her. That wasn't an excuse for stupidity, he had told her.

Taylor had stayed with Annie and her mom until she'd felt safe enough to return to her apartment. She'd somehow needed to get back into the world and reclaim a life that felt like it had crumbled around her. Annie had told her she was going through PTSD and that she should probably see someone. Instead, Taylor had quit her job at the restaurant and had taken a position as the evening front desk attendant for a twenty-four-hour gym. She befriended a couple of personal trainers and had learned everything she could about weight lifting, self-defense, and strength training. She'd spent every minute of her downtime working out until her muscles ached so much, she could barely move. Day after day, she'd pushed herself, and not only did her body meet the challenge, it had transformed. She had turned herself into the exact thing she'd needed but had lacked the night she was mugged…a weapon. And each time she worked out and pushed her body to exhaustion, she reminded herself of the vow she made. She was never going to be vulnerable again…ever.

CHAPTER FOUR

B y the time Jayden and Andy scurried the short distance from the parking lot into the old, red-brick courthouse, Jayden's face and legs were bright red from the wind biting at her exposed skin. She was cold, that was for sure, but the shaking that was rattling her insides had nothing to do with the weather. She was nervous and excited and desperately trying to remind herself to calm down. This was not real. And even though Taylor was her fairytale bride, this was not her fairytale wedding.

She glanced at Andy for a sense of grounding, and he returned a reassuring smile. He was dressed in dark purple jeans, a black turtleneck, and his fingers were hooked around a hanger sticking out from a suit bag slung over his right shoulder. Jayden wore a short blue dress with subtle peach trim under her white puffy coat, accessorized with a matching scarf wrapped twice around her neck. She'd commented several times to him yesterday that she thought it made her look like a human marshmallow.

He'd assured her that she did not, in fact, look like a walking puff of edible whipped confectionery sugar but instead looked quite sexy and fashionable. On his recommendation, she bought the coat, hoping Taylor would think the same. But it was one thing having the approval of a friend; it was quite another from someone whom she was trying to impress.

Once in the elevator, Andy pressed the appropriate button. "Take off your coat, sweetie, and let's freshen you up a bit."

"I don't want to take off my coat yet. I'm still freezing."

"Well, suck it up, buttercup. I want Taylor to see you stepping out from this elevator looking like the glamorous goddess you are. I want her jaw to drop when she sees you in your beautiful new dress."

Andy was right; it was a beautiful dress, and since Taylor had only seen Jayden in baggy sweatpants, what could it hurt modeling a little fashion on their wedding day? Especially since the dress made her feel something she hadn't felt since the accident. "Sexy," she whispered to herself. A complicated word that had been missing from her life these past few years. "Sexy," she repeated as she welcomed back a surge of confidence. It was time to show Taylor the new Jayden. "You're right, let me take this off." She pinched the coat's zipper and pulled. But halfway down, the zipper caught and tangled in the thin fabric of her dress. "Shit."

"Shit," Andy repeated as he put his suit bag down. "Here, let me do that."

The elevator dinged. As soon as the doors opened, Andy stuck his leg out to trip the sensor while he continued to pull and tug at her zipper.

"How did this happen?"

"I don't know. It just caught." Jayden's sexy feelings turned to anxiety, and it was causing her internal temperature to rise. Just once—she exhaled as she started to sweat—could she make it through a day that wasn't remembered by its cringeworthy moments? Just once! She craned her neck and took a quick sniff in the direction of her armpits. Thankfully, she still smelled of floral-citrus.

The elevator door loudly dinged its disproval at being held in place as Andy continued to try to get the zipper to release its grip on the fabric.

"Jayden?" Taylor's jaw dropped as she and another woman came upon the scene.

Andy released his grip and jumped back. Jayden's coat was pulled halfway down her arms. The front of her dress had hiked so far up her thigh, she could feel a slight breeze blow across her underwear.

"Taylor!" Jayden looked from Taylor to the other woman and back to Taylor. She had never been so embarrassed in her life. *They're laughing at me.* Her stomach soured as a feeling of nausea washed over her. Every voice in her head screamed at her to run past them and jump out the nearest window. She scanned the area for options and noticed a grand total of zero. Just solid, pale-yellow walls dimly lit with fluorescent lighting. Her wedding day was turning out to be another omen.

Feeling defeated, she reached up and uncurled the scarf from around her neck. She was burning up inside.

Taylor addressed Jayden. "We heard the elevator dinging and thought something was wrong."

Of course something's wrong, Jayden felt like screaming. Hell, why start using the word *wrong* in a sentence that referenced her existence just now? One could easily conclude her entire life was one big bundle of wrong. Her eyes began to water. All she wanted to do was crawl in a hole and die. "Nope, all's good." She awkwardly smiled as she reached to the zipper and defiantly gave it a yank. She heard the fabric rip, then saw everyone's eyebrows go up as their eyes went down.

Great, now what? She slowly glanced down, and there, sticking out through the newly made hole in her dress, was her belly button. She glanced up as a tear escaped her eye. "I swear, I'm really not this weird."

"It's true, she's not. I'm her alibi." Andy agreed. "Hi, I'm Andy." He stuck out his hand. "Man of honor, online-certified officiant, and all-round amazing guy, just…you know, throwing it out there in case you have any equally amazing single guy friends."

Taylor smiled and shook his hand. "Nice to finally meet you, Andy. This,"—Taylor cocked her head as she referenced the other woman—"is my maid of honor and best friend, Annie."

Annie turned to Jayden. "You look beautiful. Congratulations."

Andy smiled. "She is beautiful, isn't she?"

Jayden snorted. Beautiful? Really? There was nothing beautiful about someone who was a walking tragedy. Why in the world did she ever volunteer to do this? Ugh. And to think, the day had started out so hopeful.

❖

Taylor paused for a moment as she raked her eyes over Jayden. She had never seen her in anything but bulky sweats, a clean face, and hair pulled back in a ponytail. She had always considered Jayden very attractive, but now, with full makeup, hair down. and a dress that matched her baby blues, she couldn't stop staring. *Beautiful is definitely the right word to describe her.*

"Well." Taylor cleared her throat and her thoughts as she glanced down at her watch. "We better, um, go get married…you ready?"

"Yep." Jayden nodded as she placed her hand over her stomach, "I'm ready."

"Oh my God, you guys, just hearing you say that is so touching," Andy fanned his face. "I'm crying on the inside, truly crying. I don't want to ruin the two hours I spent on my makeup by crying on the outside, but trust me, inside, the tears are flowing."

"Well." Taylor smiled as she turned to Andy. "You do look fabulous."

"Thank you. Cause let me tell you…making a canvas like this"—he referenced his face—"look like a masterpiece takes time."

As they turned and walked back to the recorder's office, Taylor glanced over at him. He seemed nice, funny, and extremely supportive of Jayden. She could understand why they were best friends. "Did you bring all your paperwork?" She glanced to her left, but Jayden wasn't there. "Jayden?" She stopped and turned.

Jayden was still standing by the elevator, attempting to step out of her coat, which was now on the floor around her ankles. Taylor didn't think twice as she hustled over and wrapped a protective arm around her shoulder. And like she had done so many times in the gym, Taylor tried to ease the discomfort she sensed in Jayden.

"Oh, uh, I um…" Jayden pointed to her coat. "It wouldn't unzip anymore, so to take it off I had to, um…" Her shoulders slumped. "I don't know why I'm such a disaster today."

"Lean against me for balance."

Jayden did and was able to easily step out of the coat. Taylor continued to hold on while she bent down, scooped up the puffy fabric, and handed it to her. "Thanks," Jayden said as she took the coat and cradled it against her stomach.

"You know, I'm a bit of a nervous wreck too." She'd once told Annie that the thought of marrying someone scared her to death. She knew marriage meant loving someone enough to feel comfortable sharing her fears and vulnerabilities and trusting they would never use them against her. According to several exes, it was a level of love that she was apparently incapable of sharing. Which was exactly why she'd given up on relationships and stuck to one-night stands. They seemed to work the best because the only thing she felt obligated to share about herself was her body.

Jayden smiled. "Well, I don't think it's quite the same. I obviously represent a wrecking ball in a china shop, and you… you're the epitome of put together."

"Only on the outside."

Jayden smiled as she carefully wiped her finger under each eye, clearing the tears without smearing her mascara. "You've got one up on me because I'm a mess on the inside and outside."

"I think you look beautiful," Taylor reassured her as she cocked her head toward the others. "So what do you say we go get married?" Taylor reminded herself once again that today was about getting back at her grandfather and nothing more. But as she glanced at Jayden, she felt an unexpected tingle. The woman who she had always tried not to think too much about was definitely making an impression.

❖

Jayden stared into Taylor's sparkling, light brown eyes and thought how easy it would be to melt into her protective, sexy-as-hell arms and stay there forever.

"Yep, ready." She tapped her purse. "I've got all my paperwork right here." She broke eye contact as she took in Taylor's skin-tight black pants, equally tight white sweater, and hair molded into a perfect messy style of cuteness. Not a tux like she had envisioned and hoped for, but she'd take it. Damn, why couldn't this day be for real?

"Okay, then, let's go do this."

They filed into the office handed over the required documents and got the proper paperwork. After a quick huddle, they decided to go back to the first floor and have the ceremony inside the small atrium that sat off the main lobby.

"Figure out where you want the ceremony to take place while I go change into my priest outfit." Andy lifted his suit bag and headed to the men's room.

"Um…" Taylor spun in a slow circle. "Anyone have any preferences?"

Jayden pointed to a small section of the atrium where a banana tree and two dwarf palms were planted. "I think that area seems pretty fitting, considering."

"Perfect," Taylor agreed as they commandeered the area. They placed their coats and personal items on a wooden bench and waited for Andy to return. Jayden took the moment to grab the compact from her purse and give herself a final once-over. The made-up face reflecting back masked the emotions that stirred under the skin. She was faking more than just this marriage; she was faking her feelings. She was moments away from a lifelong fantasy, and her heart was racing. Could this turn into a Cinderella moment? Where Taylor suddenly realized how perfect they could be for each other? But deep down, she knew there would be no magical slipper moment between them. Life could sure be full of many fairytale moments, but right here and right now, this was not one of them.

"Holy shit," Annie said. "That's one hell of a priest outfit."

Andy was dressed in a skin-tight, purple, sequined jumpsuit that flared at the hems. He had on a black wig that made him look like Cher, and he wore matching purple heels. Jayden had seen him in drag more times than she could count, and each time, he looked more stunning. He sauntered up to Jayden, leaned in, and gave an air kiss to each cheek.

"You look absolutely spectacular."

"Thanks, sweetie. I thought I'd give the new outfit a test run before I wear it in the show this weekend."

"You won't disappoint."

Andy winked, spun around, and held his arms out. "Okay, ladies…I think it's time to get this party started."

Taylor smiled and cocked her head toward Jayden "He's really quite beautiful in that outfit."

"I heard that." Andy pointed to Taylor as he placed his suit bag on the bench. "And that just earned you extra friend points. Now then, shall we begin?"

Jayden's heart sped up with each step Taylor took to close the gap between them. *Easy does it.* She inhaled a shaky breath as she tried to calm herself.

"Do you have the vows?" Andy asked.

"Yeah, um…" Taylor cleared her throat as she reached in her back pocket, pulled out a small piece of paper, and handed it to him. "They're not really vows, more like a brief statement."

He unfolded the paper. "There's only one paragraph on this page." He turned the paper over, then over again, and frowned. "This is it?"

"Yeah, um, it's what I thought worked best, you know, considering the circumstances." Taylor shrugged.

Andy's face was expressionless. "I see." He cleared his throat. "Okay, then, please turn to each other and hold hands."

Taylor turned to face Jayden as she extended her hands. The moment Jayden placed her hands on top of Taylor's and squeezed, a chill shot through her, unleashing her stomach butterflies. *Oh no, no, no, not the butterflies.* Jayden had to mentally gather those pesky internal insects before they made their way to her heart. The last time that happened, she'd ended up with Carol. After that, she'd sworn she would never listen to them again; they were just a bunch of mischievous flying gremlins. But the moment Taylor smiled, she couldn't help but shiver as the butterflies tickled their way up her body.

"You okay?" Taylor asked.

"Uh-huh." She nodded and slowly let out a breath.

Andy glanced at the paper and in a dry voice said, "Today marks the day that Taylor Braxton and Jayden Wheaton agree to come together in a ceremony of marriage. Jayden, do you agree to take Taylor as your wife?"

For as long as Jayden could remember, she had always dreamed about this moment. She loved watching any and all romantic shows that ended with the characters swooning over each other and ending with the words, *I do*. Jayden's knees buckled as she prepared to say the two words that always ended in a crescendo of music and a beautiful fade-out as the characters kissed. Jayden licked her lips and said, "I do."

Andy let out a slight squeal. "Okay, and Taylor, do you agree to take Jayden as your wife?"

Taylor nodded. "I do."

"Rings, please," he said.

Taylor dug in the front pocket of her pants as Jayden retrieved the other ring from her purse and hustled back to the same position. Both she and Taylor presented identical sterling silver bands that they'd picked out at the local jeweler in the strip mall two doors down from the gym. Taylor had wanted simple and cheap, and as much as Jayden's eyes kept wandering to the set with double inlay diamonds and a brushed finish, she'd reluctantly agreed. She reminded herself there was no sense splurging for something that would only be worn a year. The ring, like the marriage, was not something she should attach meaning or feelings to. It was meant to be disposable.

"Taylor, you may now place your ring on Jayden's hand," Andy instructed.

Taylor caressed her hand and pushed the silver band onto her finger. Time slowed as Jayden became hypersensitive to the combined sensation of flesh and metal tickling its way up her finger. In its own way, those were the most erotic seconds she had felt in a long time.

"Jayden, you may now do the same," Andy said with a wave of his hand.

Jayden's hands started to shake as she slowly pushed the ring onto Taylor's finger. Her heartbeat accelerated to over-caffeinated levels, the atrium felt like it jumped twenty degrees, and damn it, the butterflies got out of their cage again and were wreaking havoc in her stomach.

"By the power vested in me"—Andy looked up from the paper—"as a fabulous-looking ordained minister, I pronounce you married. You may now kiss the other bride."

Jayden licked her lips. But after an awkward moment of Taylor standing frozen, she sighed, leaned in, and gave her a quick hug. So much for the romantic movie ending.

Andy rolled his eyes. "Or that."

Taylor walked to the wooden bench and picked up the marriage license. "Do you have a pen, Jayden?" She signed the document, handed it to Annie, then to Jayden, and finally over to Andy. "Last signature's yours."

"I feel so important." Andy took the pen and signed. "Guess it's on me to turn this bad boy back in. Congratulations, ladies, looks like you're officially married." He hugged Taylor, then turned to Jayden and gave her a huge squeeze. "I love you so much, sweetie, and I'm so happy for you."

Jayden whispered back, "I love you too. You better come visit."

Andy pulled away. "I'm way ahead of you. I've already bought three pairs of board shorts and the cutest flip-flops you've ever seen."

Jayden laughed as Taylor approached. "Annie and I are going out for drinks. You guys wanna come?"

Andy looked at Jayden and subtly nodded. She knew he was signaling that he was up for it, but she didn't feel like going out, at least not with Taylor and Annie. A bittersweet feeling washed over her, and a bit of melancholy settled in. She didn't want to celebrate something that was just a business arrangement. Instead, she wanted to let what just transpired settle inside her and allow her own fantasies around it play out. "No, my leg's not feeling all that great from standing so much," she mumbled. "I think I better get home and relax, but thanks anyway."

Taylor nodded. "All right, then, well, I guess I'll see you at the airport in a couple weeks."

"Yep, see you there." She smiled as Taylor and Annie gathered their coats and walked out of the building.

Andy folded his arms across his chest. "Is your leg really hurting, or was that bullshit?"

She shrugged.

"Tell you what," Andy said as he motioned for her to lift her arms so he could slide her coat over her head. "We look too fabulous to go straight home. Why don't we go to Bernie's and do our own celebrating? Some of the guys said they'd be there tonight, and I want to show off my new look."

Bernie's was a small men's bar that he liked to frequent. The place was low-key and set up more like a coffee house than a bar. Jayden had always felt comfortable and welcome there.

"Deal. But only if we swing by the house so I can change. I'm not going out with you looking so glamorous and me in a dress with a hole ripped out of the center."

"That's my girl." He kissed her cheek. "Now, why don't you sit down for a moment while I go turn this license in?"

She nodded, grabbed the side arm of the bench, and slowly sank into its wooden seat. She pulled her phone out and took the moment to scroll through her predictable social media feed. She thought about changing her status to married but decided against it. In a year, she would have to change it back to single and deal with a barrage of sympathy comments and questions. All of them would be unwelcome. She didn't ask for anyone's opinion when she made this decision, and she wouldn't need it in the end. For once in her life, she was going with her gut instinct and hoping it wouldn't steer her off a cliff.

"Ready?" Andy grabbed his suit bag, and flung it over his shoulder. "Come now, Mrs. Jayden Wheaton-Braxton, your chariot awaits."

Mrs. Jayden Wheaton-Braxton. The title would be short-lived, but it made her smile nonetheless.

The date was February second, her wedding day. It was also the day the divorce clock started ticking. This time next year, the deed to the Maui property would be in Taylor's hand, and their divorce would soon follow. She twirled her wedding band. She liked the way it felt on her finger. Maybe she would ask Taylor if she could keep it as a souvenir after they'd divorced.

Divorce. Jayden snorted. It felt so weird to be in a marriage where the exact day she was getting divorced was predetermined. Oh well. She shrugged as she followed Andy out of the courthouse. If only all of life were that predictable.

CHAPTER FIVE

Jayden activated her phone screen, checked the time and was disappointed that only five minutes had elapsed since the last time she checked it. *Come on.* She fidgeted as she rubbed her thigh. She needed to get off the plane and stretch her leg before it locked up. She shifted her weight back and forth, pulled at her jeans, craned her neck out the window for signs of land, and checked her phone again. Only another ten minutes of her life had ticked by.

She threw her head against the seat and closed her eyes. She needed to relax. She took a few deep breaths, then flopped her head to the side. Taylor was sitting in the middle seat next to her, a bright green travel pillow wrapped around her neck. She had been asleep the entire flight, and Jayden was envious. She regretted not taking her doctor up on his offer for sleeping pills.

As she watched Taylor sleep, her envy turned to jealousy. *What did she do last night that made her so tired?* She envisioned Taylor being out with her friends partying the night away. Or maybe she had a one-night stand to celebrate her move to Hawaii? That thought burned through Jayden, and she had to check herself. This marriage was a no-strings-attached deal, and that meant both were free to be the person they wanted to be without interference from the other. She had no claim over Taylor. None. Baby crush or not, they were friends, and as such, free to do their own thing.

A crackle sounded over the PA system, followed by the announcement that they'd be landing soon. "Finally," she mumbled as she placed her hand on Taylor's forearm. "Hey, we're landing."

❖

Taylor blinked her eyes open, stretched as much as physically possible in a center seat with personal items tangled around her feet, and leaned across Jayden to look out the window. The island was not yet in view, but she could clearly see the white caps in the water.

"Looks beautiful." She rubbed her eyes. The sun sparkled across the ocean's surface like glistening diamonds. Such a welcome sight after gray skies, dirty snow, and bare trees.

"And warm," Jayden threw out.

"Yes." Taylor yawned. "And warm."

She had been logging close to zero hours of sleep the past few days as she closed down her life. She gave notice at the gym, paid the ridiculous fee for an early lease termination to her apartment complex, and packed and shipped anything that had sentimental value to the B and B in Maui. Everything else, she sold.

In a way, she was glad to get rid of so much of her former life. A life that had not only held heartache and financial struggle, but brought the nightmares that continued to haunt her to this day. She had thought by now that she would be free of them, but no such luck. They could still rear up at any moment and chase her into dark corners of her mind. She was hoping the move to Maui would help with that. That the nightmares would somehow be left behind with everything else she had walked away from.

"Sorry I slept the whole flight. I didn't get any sleep last night." She yawned again as the memory of her evening flashed in her mind. She had asked Annie if she would set aside the night for the two of them because she needed to talk to her about a few things. They'd met at an Italian restaurant close to Taylor's apartment, and halfway through dinner, she had pulled a yellow envelope out of her backpack and slid it across the table.

"What's this?" Annie mumbled through a mouthful of ziti as she gave Taylor a suspicious look.

"Just open it." Taylor smiled.

Annie ripped open the flap and pulled out a card. "To the best friend anyone could ask for," she read. "Aww." She clutched the card to her chest.

"Open it," Taylor instructed as she chewed her spaghetti.

Annie did, and a check floated out and landed on her lap. She picked up the check and gasped. "Is this real?"

"Very."

Annie looked over at Taylor and cocked her head, "I don't understand."

"That's the money I got from selling my grandfather's condo. I want you to have it." Last year, Annie had moved her mother into her apartment and had begun caring for her after her mom slipped on a patch of ice and broke her hip. The medical bills and rehab costs were more than her mom could cover, so Annie had stepped in, cleaned out her own savings account, and even that barely made a dent in the bills.

"That should cover what's left of your mom's medical bills, with enough left over for you to put a down payment on a house." Taylor dug into her backpack again, pulled out a keychain that had two identical keys on it, and slid it over to Annie. "Those are the keys to grandpa's minivan. It's basically brand-new and has all the bells and whistles. It's yours now."

"Taylor—"

"No, Annie. You need a minivan to take your mom to all her appointments. This thing can handle her wheelchair, and the seats sit up high, so it'll be easier for her to get in and out."

"I can't take these." Annie placed the keys on the check and slid them back over to Taylor.

"I want you to have them. You guys are family to me, and I know how much the money and car can help you both. I want you to take them. Please, for me." Taylor couldn't remember a time in her life when Annie and her mom weren't there for her. They had been there in the good times and the bad. No matter how unstable she felt, they were always a constant. And now, for the first time in her life, she finally had something to give back. And she took pride in that thought.

Annie regarded her as tears welled in her eyes. "You're right, it would make the world of difference. But are you sure?"

"Positive."

Annie slid out of the booth and slid in next to Taylor. She wrapped her arms around her and held her for several minutes while they both cried. "I love you, you know." Annie wiped her eyes. "And I'm going to miss you like crazy."

"I love you too." Taylor leaned away. "And I expect both of you to come visit me."

"We will." Annie sniffed as she rubbed the tears off her cheek. "It's going to be lonely without you."

"I'll check in with you every day." Taylor reassured her as the reality of the move was settling in. For the first time in her life, she was going to be truly on her own, and that thought was a bit frightening. "And if anything happens and you need me to come home, I'll be on the next flight out. Now let's finish up here, put in an order for your mom, and spend the night watching movies at your place."

"Wouldn't you rather spend your last night here at the bar?"

Taylor held up her hand. "I'm a married woman."

Annie laughed. "Yeah, right."

Taylor placed her arms around Annie again and squeezed. "You know the only place I want to be tonight is with you two."

"Then an all-nighter with movies and popcorn it is."

"Sounds wonderful." Taylor would not miss the bar scene or this town. In fact, the only emotional tie that had kept her rooted in Missouri was Annie and her mom. They gave her the one thing she had yet to find in a relationship. A safe place to be herself.

The jolt from the wheels hitting the runway brought Taylor back from her thoughts. She was already missing Annie. They had never been geographically separated. The adjustment was going to take time.

The second the plane parked at the gate, Jayden unbuckled her seat belt and stood. She placed all her weight on her good leg as she rubbed her bad one.

"How's your leg?" Taylor asked as they waited their turn.

"The change in position is definitely a welcome relief." Jayden groaned. "Hopefully by the time we get to baggage claim, it'll stop its unbearable ache and return to its usual dull throbbing."

"Let me know if you need anything," Taylor said as she stepped into the aisle. She had spent years turning her body into a machine so that it would serve her. She couldn't imagine what it would be like if an accident took that away. The thought of having to rely on others for help was unsettling.

"I will. Thanks Taylor, I appreciate that."

They made their way through the terminal and waited for their luggage, mingling around the many brochure racks advertising everything from scuba diving lessons to luaus. It took thirty minutes before they grabbed their luggage. They headed to the restroom, stripped off their heavy sweaters, and changed into T-shirts.

They followed the signs to the rental car tram, and an hour later, Taylor hoisted their luggage in the back of a Jeep, typed the address of the B and B in her phone, and hit go. She threw the car into drive, glanced at Jayden, and smiled. She had no idea what was waiting for her, but as she pulled out of the parking lot, one thing was for sure, her life would never be the same.

A soft female voice guided them across the narrow portion of the island to the southwest shores of Kihei. Twenty-five minutes later when they'd arrived, she thought there was a mistake. They were on a small back road without a house in sight.

"Are you sure you typed in the right address?" Jayden asked.

"Yeah, I'm pretty sure." Taylor scanned the area for any signs of a bed and breakfast but didn't see anything. Anxiety gripped her. She had just given up everything to come to a place sight unseen. What if this whole thing was just a sick joke to get her to marry? What if there really wasn't a B and B?

"There," Jayden said as she pointed to a red mailbox sticking halfway out of the thick and overgrown foliage.

Taylor eased the Jeep forward. She checked the address on the mailbox. "Yep, this is it." She slowly turned into a narrow gravel driveway and followed it through a natural canopy of trees and bushes full of a variety of multicolored flowers. She had never seen such an incredible display of floral beauty. "Wow." She whispered as a twinge of sadness stabbed at her heart. Her mom would have loved to see this.

"I smell the ocean."

Taylor tilted her head and took in a deep breath. The distinctive briny smell made her smile. "Me too."

"Oh. My. God." Jayden gasped as the foliage cleared, and an old, two-story house with pale yellow siding and a wraparound porch presented itself. A beautiful, manicured lawn that stretched twenty yards separated the beach from the house, and thirty yards beyond that was the ocean. "It's beautiful."

Through the corner of her eye, Taylor could see Jayden beaming with joy. She looked like the epitome of pure happiness, and watching her reaction was heartwarming. "Yeah, no kidding," Taylor said as she pulled up next to a beat-up black compact car that was parked where the driveway morphed into a space that could easily accommodate a half dozen cars.

As soon as Taylor put the Jeep in park and cut the engine, a large Polynesian man in his early thirties, long hair pulled back in a ponytail, cargo shorts that hung to his knees, worn-in flip-flops, and a traditional Hawaiian shirt, bolted out of the sliding front doors of the house.

Taylor hopped out. "I'm Taylor Braxton. You must be Sam?" Michael had informed her that upon Frank's passing, the property's fulltime chef and handyman was to stay on and continue to be paid in full until the deed was reassigned to a new owner. "He lives inland with his grandmother." Michael had told her, as if that was an endorsement for his continued employment. But something wasn't adding up. Her grandfather had never been a generous person, so keeping Sam on the payroll seemed odd. Why had Frank extended to him the one thing she had always craved but never received? His affection.

"Aloha." Sam opened his arms, but Taylor stepped back. Hugs came only after trust was earned, and right now, she wasn't sure if Sam was trustworthy. Anyone that seemed to have a better relationship with her grandfather than she or her mom did was instantly suspicious. She extended her arm, and Sam gently shook it.

Jayden slowly flopped out of her side of the Jeep and limped over. "Hi, Sam, I'm Jayden."

Sam extended his hand, but Jayden leaned in and gave him a warm embrace. Taylor had always noticed Jayden's sense of ease around strangers. And unlike her, Jayden openly welcomed people into her personal space. It was one of many things she found so intriguing about her.

"Here, let me help you with your bags." He pulled their luggage out. "I have the master bedroom all ready for you."

"Thanks. What's that over there?" Taylor nodded to a small house that sat on the edge of the property amongst several tall hibiscus shrubs.

"It's a cottage. Your grandfather built it about twenty years ago. One of his friend's wives decorated it, so as you'll see, it looks nothing like the house."

"Why'd he build it?" Jayden chimed in.

"Frank didn't like any kids running around the main house, so he had the cottage built for friends who brought their families here to stay. But this place hasn't had any guests for quite a while, so the cottage, as well as all the upstairs rooms, have been empty for years."

That piece of news startled Taylor. She'd just assumed the place was a working B and B, and she would be taking over an operation that was already set up and running. "Why?" She asked as she looked over the outside of the house. It was a bit weathered and in need of a fresh coat of paint, but other than that, it seemed in good shape. From the outside, everything looked to be in working order. So why no guests?

"You'll see." He hoisted the suitcases up the two steps, then rolled them across the wooden deck and into the house.

"Oh, wow," Jayden whispered as she crinkled her nose.

Taylor stood stunned as she looked at the huge painting of a World War II bomber in a dramatic action scene that graced the main wall of the small entryway. What was her grandfather's obsession with the war? She shook her head in disgust as she turned to Jayden. "He had a thing for war."

"Oh, that's nothing, just wait till you see the rest of the place. Come on, I'll give you the tour." Sam cocked his head and led the way.

Behind the entryway wall to the right was the kitchen, and to the left was the sitting room. A small hallway off the sitting room led to a decent-sized master bedroom and full bath. The other downstairs bathroom was a half bath that was nestled under the stairway that led to three bedrooms on the second floor, as well as an additional two full bathrooms. Smoke-stained brown paneling graced every wall, and the furniture, although beautifully crafted, was right out of the 1950s. The appliances looked about twenty years old, and the only thing Taylor saw from this decade was the large flat-screen mounted on the wall in the living room. Grandpa loved to watch his football. A bitter memory of her as a child begging for his attention and being scolded for interrupting his game watching, flashed in her head. Sadly, she had learned at a young age that there were things in his life that would always take precedence over her.

"Everything in here is so outdated." She frowned.

"Your grandfather bought this house after the war, and he prided himself on keeping it just as it was when he bought it. And he would only let World War II or Korean War vets stay here. That's why the place has been struggling for a while. The clientele has pretty much died off."

Taylor snorted. "You've got to be shitting me."

Sam shook his head. "I kept telling him to expand his parameters, but he would shake his head and dig in his heels. He said he didn't want any riff-raff in his place, just his kind."

Taylor pinched the bridge of her nose. "That sounds like something my grandfather would say." She remembered the embarrassment of being in public with him. Seemed there wasn't a person he encountered who didn't irritate him. Why should his comment about riff-raff even shock her?

"Yeah, he was…" Sam paused as he seemed to carefully choose his next word. "Interesting." He led them to the kitchen. "Are you hungry? I can make you a burger."

"I understand you're quite the chef and handyman," Taylor said.

He let out a charming laugh. "Who told you that? I can cook a mean burger and heat up fries, if that constitutes as chef skills. As far as being a handyman, I can unclog a toilet, if that's what you mean." He walked over to the refrigerator and opened the freezer. It was packed full of frozen meat and bags of potato fries. "The only thing your grandfather wanted to eat while he was here was burgers and fries. That's it. All day, every day. And weirdly, when his military friends came to stay, so did they. They all thought it was great."

"That's gross." Jayden wrinkled her nose.

Sam shrugged. "Not my food of choice, but hey, I did what Frank wanted."

"Is there any other food in the house? I am getting kinda hungry, and I don't really want a burger or fries." Taylor pulled out one of six, sea-foam-green Formica chairs and sat at the chrome table. The setting looked cool, in a retro kind of way, and she decided she kind of liked it.

Sam opened the other side of the refrigerator, and it was fully stocked with beer cans. "As you can see, your grandfather had limited taste. But fear not, while you guys get settled in, I'll go over to my buddy's place that's right around the corner. They make the best ono fish tacos you've ever had. I'll get their large takeout."

Taylor reached in her back pocket and pulled out her wallet. She unfolded it and pulled out three twenties. "Will that cover it?"

Sam scooped up the bills from the counter and shoved them in his front pocket. "That'll more than cover it. Since my buddy owns the place, I get a discount."

As he walked out the front door, Taylor leaned against the kitchen counter and turned to Jayden. "I was thinking, one of us could take the cottage house and the other the master bedroom. Which would you like?" Since her growing attraction toward Jayden was beginning to fuel desires, she thought it best if they lived apart instead of under the same roof. She didn't need the temptation.

"Why don't I take the cottage? That way, you can stay in here and get a better feel for what you want to do to the house. I can already see your wheels spinning."

"That obvious, huh?"

"Well, I mean, just look at this place."

"Yeah, my grandpa thought the world revolved around two things, the military and himself. Come on." Taylor pushed off the kitchen counter. "Let's go check out the cottage and get you settled in."

They worked their way back around walls and corners until they were once again in the entryway. Taylor grabbed Jayden's suitcase and wheeled it behind her as they made their way across the lawn and over to the cottage. As soon as she opened the door, she smiled.

❖

"Wow," Jayden said as she limped past her.

The design was open and simple. A great room greeted them as they stepped inside. The kitchen was to the left, master bedroom to the right, and straight ahead was a beautiful view of the ocean. The walls were painted a light blue pastel, the shutters were basic white, and the place was decorated in a tropical theme.

"I love it," Jayden said. Everything about the cottage spoke to her. The pastel color scheme, the open feel, and the Hawaiian vibe. There was something about the place that instantly touched her soul and made her feel relaxed, comfortable and at home.

"Then for the next year, it's yours,"

Jayden fluttered around the cottage. Hearing the words, *it's yours* made her want to reach out and hug Taylor, but instead, she just turned to her and smiled. "Thanks." Jayden cringed on the inside. Why was it so easy to hug Sam and not Taylor? Because her attraction to Taylor was becoming harder and harder to ignore, and an intimate embrace might betray her feelings. *Besides, we're just friends and this is just business.* She hoped if she repeated that statement enough, it would override her desires, but she was beginning to doubt that.

"Well, then, I'll let you unpack and settle in."

Jayden nodded, thanked her two more times, and as soon as Taylor left, she took several pictures and sent them to Andy. Her phone chimed, displaying a heart, palm tree, and ocean wave emoji.

Halfway into unpacking, Jayden's phone chimed again to let her know Sam was back with dinner. She limped to her purse and grabbed her bottle of pain pills. She made her way into the kitchen and downed two pills. The day had been a long one, and her travel high was giving way to fatigue, hunger, and body aches.

As she crossed the lawn to the main house, she stopped to look at the setting sun. The orange glow was reflecting in the water, and Jayden was convinced that no human artist would ever be able to capture its true beauty. After snapping several pictures and sending a few to Andy, she turned and hobbled up the front porch steps one at a time.

She was in paradise, she was warm, and she lived in the cutest little cottage she had ever seen. She wasn't sure what she had done in her life to deserve this, but whatever it was, she was grateful. Maybe she would still have her Cinderella moment? After all, the ball was just beginning, and she was a year away from the stroke of midnight. She smiled at the thought as she entered the house. A girl could dream, couldn't she?

CHAPTER SIX

Jayden bolted upright in bed. Her heart was beating rapidly, and she gasped for breath. She quickly took in her surroundings as she tried to calm herself. *Where am I?* Fragmented pictures from yesterday flashed through her mind. "The cottage," she mumbled as her breathing began to return to normal.

She was not in her car, spinning through the intersection, but safe in the cottage. It was just another nightmare. She exhaled the thought as she glanced at the clock and frowned. Five in the morning. Earlier than she wanted to get up, but she was too wired to go back to sleep. Screw it. She flung her legs over the side of the bed and reached for the pill bottle on her nightstand. She downed two pills and decided to go outside and catch some fresh air.

She didn't bother changing out of her pink flamingo pajama bottoms and white V-neck T-shirt. It was so early in the morning, who would she possibly run into? She hit the flashlight icon on her phone, grabbed a lounge chair from the porch, and drug it over to where the grass and sand became one. She plopped down in the green padding. The sun would not rise for another thirty minutes, so she tried to relax in the darkness and focus on the sound of waves crashing against the shore. A cool breeze blew over her body, and as she breathed in the salty air, she wondered again how she got so lucky. She considered texting her dad and letting him know she would be in Maui for the next year but placed that thought on a mental Post-it and put it in her *things to get around to* pile.

Years ago, her dad had taken a job transfer and had moved to Canada with wife number three, also known as his secretary. Such a cliché. Jayden had met her once at a barbeque at her dad's house. They were all over each other, and she had found it embarrassing to be around. Thoughts about what her dad did in bed were gross enough. Seeing it play out in front of her was more than she wanted to deal with. She'd ended up cutting that evening short and had declined his next two invitations. A voice mail let her know they had moved to Toronto, and Jayden had no intension of ever visiting. Her relationship with him was strained at best and nonexistent at most. After her mom had caught him cheating with the woman who'd eventually become wife number two, she'd filed for divorce. But before her parents could rip each other apart in divorce court, her mom had died of an aneurysm. Jayden was convinced it was stress induced, and she put all the blame on her father.

On second thought… Jayden set her phone down on the lounge chair. *I don't think I'll tell him anything.* He'd never know the difference, and trying to explain the circumstances of her marriage to Taylor would only bring up unwanted questions and unwelcome replies.

Jayden took another deep breath of clean seaside air, calmed any lingering thoughts of her dad, and twirled the ring on her finger, setting off a chill of excitement that tickled its way up her spine. Funny how an inanimate object could elicit such a strong emotion. Jayden sank deeper in the chair and closed her eyes as she let her mind settle.

She woke again to sunshine and the sound of heavy breathing as Taylor jogged barefoot in the sand toward her. *God, that woman's body is amazing.* Jayden focused on the water droplets glistening off Taylor's brown arms and legs. She wore tight black running shorts and a red and black sports bra. Jayden chewed at her lower lip as Taylor made her way to the lounge chair and stood over her.

Taylor tapped her watch, then bent and placed her hands on her knees as she took a moment to catch her breath.

"How long have you been, um, jogging?" Jayden stumbled as she stared at Taylor's breasts for way longer than she should. But damn it, when a beautiful woman bent down in front of her, and they were just right there in her face, what was she supposed to do?

"A little...over...an hour. I'm not used to...running on sand, and I can really feel it in my calves." Taylor huffed as she stood and began shaking out her legs. "I woke up early and couldn't get back to sleep, so I figured I might as well go for a run."

"And the first thought I had when I woke up was to grab a lounge chair and sit my ass down."

Taylor smiled. "Actually, that looks wonderful. Let me grab a chair and join you." She jogged to the porch, grabbed a lounge chair, and pulled it next to Jayden.

"How are you not totally exhausted?"

Taylor plopped down. "I pretty much crashed after dinner. But when I woke up to pee, I couldn't get back to sleep. My head was spinning a mile a minute, so I just gave up trying and came out here." After a moment of peaceful silence, she flopped her head to the side. "Kind of nice, isn't it?"

"Never in a million dreams did I think I would be living in a beach cottage on Maui."

"I know. Never in a million dreams did I think I would inherit one. I'll never understand why my grandfather didn't tell us about this place. My mom would have loved it here."

Jayden couldn't imagine growing up with a grandfather who seemed to consciously choose to turn his back on his entire family. "Your grandfather was a real ass, huh?"

Taylor frowned. "Yeah. although there were times when he could be halfway decent, but those were few and far between. Most of the time he was distant, angry, critical, and condescending. He could lash out at the drop of a hat for no apparent reason. I think I spent my entire life walking on eggshells around him."

"That sounds awful."

"It was worse for my mom. Grandpa raised her with a heavy hand, she said, which I think was code for him smacking her around, but she never came out and said that. When she was seventeen, she ran away with a boy one town over and got pregnant with me. When she eventually told him, he threw her out of the house."

"Holy shit," Jayden whispered.

"Yeah, and the boy's parents moved out of state before Mom could tell him, so I never knew my dad."

Jayden nodded as she thought again about her father. Yes, they were estranged, and yes, she blamed him for her mother's death. But deep down, she always knew that if she ever really needed him, he would be there for her, and she took comfort in that thought.

"I never met my grandfather until I was five. And even after he came back into our lives, he never once offered to help us out in any way…not once."

"Damn, that's coldhearted."

Taylor shrugged. "I guess you can't miss something you never had. That's why turning the tables on him makes me feel—"

The sound of Sam's car sputtering down the driveway interrupted her. Taylor glanced at her watch. "He gets here early."

Sam had on a pair of cargo shorts that looked exactly like the ones he was wearing yesterday, a blue T-shirt that had MAUI written across the chest, and he was clutching a white paper bag.

"Hey, Sam," Jayden called and waved. "We're over here."

Sam turned and smiled. He grabbed a lounge chair off the porch and joined them. "Aloha, ladies. I see you're already getting into the relaxing vibe of the island."

"I am," Jayden replied. "That one, however"—she pointed to Taylor—"already ran a marathon this morning."

Taylor snorted. "More like a slow 10K."

"By choice or was something chasing you?" Sam teased.

Jayden giggled. "My people." She put her hand up, and Sam high-fived it.

"I come bearing gifts." He reached in the bag and pulled out scones. "My buddy's family owns a bakery not far from here. This morning's special was pineapple coconut."

"Holy shit." Jayden moaned as she bit into the pastry. "These are amazing."

"So," Sam mumbled as he chewed, "what's the plan for today, boss?"

"Well, I've been really giving this some thought. I think I'd like to do a full makeover of the house, you know, tear down walls and everything. I want to turn the place into a gay B and B."

Jayden sat upright. "Taylor, that would be awesome."

"I was thinking about it when I was running, and it would be a nice way to kinda stick it to my grandfather. Since he was so homophobic, why not turn the little hideaway he seemed to love more than his family into the gayest place on Maui?"

Sam threw his head back and laughed. "Taylor, I like your style. Frank could sure be—"

"Sexiest, raciest, homophobic, a total ass. Am I missing anything?"

Sam smiled. "I think that covers it."

"Then, unfortunately, we knew the same man. How good are you at remodeling?"

He shook his head. "I'm not, but I could round up some buddies who do construction."

"How soon?"

"I can start making calls right away."

"I'll need bids and estimates."

"Yeah, no problem."

Taylor raised her scone. "To the gayest B and B on the island."

"Hear, hear," Jayden smiled as she raised what was left of her pastry in the air. A gay B and B was an awesome idea. But as she listened to Taylor talk in detail about her vision, she felt a touch of melancholy settle in. Taylor was making plans for a future that did not include her. And rightly so. This was not about her. She was just someone passing through. A means to an end. But the more she listened, the more she reflected on her own life. She thought about her own long-term plans and realized she didn't have any. No goals, no aspirations, nothing. Since the accident, all she'd thought about was just trying to get through life one day at a time. She had been existing but not living.

Hmm, she thought as she looked at the sun sparkling on the water. Maybe it was time she started thinking about renovating her own life. She was long overdue for a makeover.

❖

Jayden spent the next four hours walking around the exterior and interior of the property with Taylor and Sam. She took mental notes as Taylor threw out idea after idea about how she wanted to transform the place. Everyone agreed all the wall paneling needed to go, but the original hardwood floors should remain. Taylor singled out the four walls on the lower level to tear down that would allow the entry, kitchen, and living room to become one large great room. She wanted to replace and update all the appliances, kitchen cabinets, and countertops, and remodel all bathrooms and buy new furniture. After deciding on a color scheme for all the rooms, Taylor gave Jayden the task of getting online and ordering gay trinkets, flags, windsocks, posters, stickers, statues, and household knick-knacks. Anything to "gay up" the place.

Jayden sat on the couch hunched over her laptop when Taylor plopped down beside her. "Finding some good stuff?"

"I think it would be fair to say your grandfather will be rolling in his grave." Although Jayden had never met Frank, she guessed that she would have found the man repulsive. Being a part of transforming his precious little bed and breakfast into a glamorous gay getaway was not only something she was relishing, it came with an unexpected perk. A welcome opportunity to work side by side with Taylor.

"Good, because I want this place to scream gay."

"Oh, it will."

"Ladies?" Sam came up behind them holding three pairs of snorkel masks and two sets of fins. A rolled-up beach towel sat under his arm. "Who wants to take a break?"

Taylor smiled. "Where did you get those?"

"A buddy of mine works at a snorkel shop. He let me have them for a couple of days." He placed them on the coffee table.

"Is there anyone on this island who isn't your buddy?" Jayden asked.

He shrugged. "I have a lot of friends." He placed his beach towel on the coffee table, unrolled it, and pulled out a pair of board shorts. "I'm going to change, be right back."

"Sounds like a plan." Jayden closed her laptop. "I'll throw on my suit and meet you back here." She got up and headed to the cottage. Fifteen minutes later, she was in her black one-piece suit under a pair of baggy, pastel-orange board shorts.

"Everyone ready?" Sam walked out of the kitchen tying a small white scuba mesh bag that contained three heads of lettuce around his waist.

Jayden eyed the bag. "Does lunch come with this outing?"

"This is for Charlotte, our resident honu. If you're lucky, you'll get to meet her today."

"What's a honu?"

"It's a turtle," Taylor answered as she grabbed the gear off the coffee table.

"How do you know that?"

"I saw a beach towel at one of the stores at the airport that had a picture of a sea turtle and the word honu written below it."

Sam laughed. "You'll need to expand your native vocabulary beyond what you see on beach towels."

"I'm counting on you for tutorials," Taylor said as Jayden shuffled behind them. She thought how cool it would be to learn the language, but then reminded herself again that she was not here to stay. She was only a temporary placeholder until Taylor received the deed. And as she listened to Sam patiently teach Taylor a few words in Hawaiian, she felt a twinge of discomfort as she realized she was the odd one out.

"Okay," Sam said as he stopped a few yards from the water. "It's probably best if you sit and put your fins on here, then walk backward into the water."

Taylor and Jayden plopped down on the sand, slipped the fins on their bare feet, and adjusted the straps.

"Where are your fins?" She glanced over at Sam.

"I don't wear them unless I'm out free diving with my buddies."

"Oh," Jayden grunted as she struggled to stand. Sam rushed to her side, reached out a hand, and effortlessly pulled her to her feet.

"Thanks Sam," she said as she steadied herself. She was grateful for the help but frustrated that after a year of trying to rebuild her strength in the gym, she still had to rely on others for support.

"Okay," Sam said, "now take your mask and put it on your face and make sure it's tight enough but not too tight. And that the mouthpiece of the snorkel feels comfortable."

A few slight adjustments later, they gave the thumbs-up that they were all set and ready to go.

"Okay, now, I'll hold on to you while you walk backward into the surf. When you get about waist deep, I'll let you go, and then you just turn and dive on in."

Taylor and Jayden turned as he hooked one arm around Jayden, but as he reached for Taylor, she jerked away and motioned that she was fine without his assistance. "You just concentrate on Jayden, I'm good."

Jayden glanced at Taylor and wondered what about Sam seemed to set her off at times. One minute, Taylor could be talking and laughing with him, and the next, she seemed repulsed by him.

A few steps into the water, a wave crashed into her, and she stumbled. Sam tightened his grip. "I've got you." *Touch,* Jayden realized. Taylor doesn't want to be touched. As she turned and watched her dive into the water, she curiously wondered, *What happened to you?*

With Sam's help, Jayden safely turned and dove into the ocean. Sam followed her. He swam in close proximity and asked if they were okay by signaling a thumbs-up. The water was clear, the visibility was good, and the fish were everywhere. Within minutes, Jayden and Taylor were tapping each other's shoulders as they pointed to the beauty that surrounded them. Goose bumps tingled up her skin as her body responded to being immersed in a world of vibrant simmering colors. She was awestruck. For twenty minutes, they swam back and forth, mesmerized at the wonders of the ocean. Sam became their aquatic tour guide as he told them what they were looking at. He pointed to the Humuhumunukunukuapua'a, Hawaii's state fish, with its distinctive thick black stripe that masked the fish's eyes and ran the length of its yellowish body. He pointed out a small blueish octopus trying to hide amongst some rocks, and he reminded them to look up so they could see the transparent looking needlefish that swam just under the surface.

Jayden couldn't remember a time when she'd felt so completely captivated by her surroundings. So utterly mesmerized by life in general. She felt giddy, almost euphoric as she took in the lifeforms around her. An entire world of wonder lay just under the surface, completely unseen by the naked eye. It made her sad that she had never been snorkeling before. There was amazing life and beauty beyond words that she had been missing out on because she had only experienced the world from above the water. Being a land dweller wasn't all it was cracked up to be.

She bobbed in the water and hovered over a school of florescent yellow fish. She appreciated the water's buoyancy effortlessly holding up her body as the waves slowly rocked her back and forth. The sun felt warm on her back, and she was so relaxed, it took her a moment to register the huge shadow that was moving closer to her.

Get out of the water now, her mind screamed as it raced with horrific images of great white shark attacks. She squealed and slapped her arms and fins on the surface as she propelled her way back to the beach. As she tensed up, pain shot through her leg, and she became convinced the shark had hold of her. Her heartbeat pounded in her head, and breathing through her snorkel felt suffocating as she tried to gasp for more air.

I'm going to die! With one final burst of adrenaline, she kicked out. A moment later, she hit shallow water. She stood and tried to run to shore, but a wave crashed into her and sent her tumbling, legs dangling in the air, arms flaying, until the ocean deposited her on the beach. She lay on her back, water ebbing and flowing around her as she coughed. Her leg was on fire as the muscles cramped. She moaned in agony as she slowly turned over, coughed some more, then tried to stumble to her feet, but her leg collapsed under her, sending her to face-plant into the sand. She cried out and spit out sand and water.

"Jayden?" Taylor called. "What happened?"

Jayden sat upright and pointed behind them "Shadow." She spit more sand out of her mouth. "Huge shadow." She coughed. "Man-eating big shadow."

"That's Charlotte," Sam said in a calm voice as a five-foot-long green sea turtle broke the surface. He retrieved a piece of lettuce and handed it to her. She gently took it in her beaklike mouth and began chomping on it.

"That's Charlotte?" Jayden mumbled as she rubbed the cramping pain out of her leg. The adrenaline surging through her veins just moments ago was instantly replaced with embarrassment. The crushing sensation of being the odd one out reared its head again. "When you said turtle," she called, "I thought you meant a cute little thing." She held her hands about eight inches apart as she watched Taylor and Sam interact with Charlotte.

Taylor waved. "Come on back in."

Oh, hell no. Jayden glanced up and waved back as she took off her fins. "No, I'm good." She picked globs of sand from her swimsuit and watched Charlotte gracefully swim around Sam and Taylor in what looked like an affectionate manner. Sam handed a piece of lettuce to Taylor, who fed it to Charlotte. The look on her face was so bright. Jayden couldn't recall a time when Taylor had smiled that big and this often. The more she watched Taylor and Sam interact with the sea turtle, the more enticing it became. She was missing out on a wonderful moment with Taylor, and that thought bothered her.

She slowly stumbled to her feet. *You've got this.* She said the words that kept her going in the gym every time she wanted to quit. *You've got this.* Before Jayden knew it, she was back in the water and going toward the magical interaction with this sea creature.

Sam and Taylor were only a few yards out, and by the time she slowly paddled over to them, the stabbing sensation in her leg had subsided. The buoyancy of the water seemed to be working its magic, and once again she decided the aquatic life resonated with her.

"Wanna feed her?" Sam asked as he held out a piece of lettuce.

"Um." Jayden hesitated.

"She's gentle, she would never harm you." Sam said in a soft calming voice.

As soon as Jayden took the leaf, her heart rate increased with both excitement and fear. She steadied herself as much as possible and extended her arm as far as it would go. She placed the lettuce at the tip of her fingers and held her breath as Charlotte closed the gap between them and grabbed the leaf.

Jayden flinched at first, but as soon as she heard Taylor's reassuring words tell her how great she'd done, a sense of accomplishment washed over her. Not that feeding a sea turtle took much effort. It was more the sense that Taylor understood she was trying to overcome a fear, and like so many times in the gym, Taylor's encouragement and praise got her through.

As Charlotte finished off the last of the leaf, Jayden took the time to marvel at her massive, intimidating girth and gentle demeanor. The turtle was beautiful and graceful, and by the time Jayden had fed her a second piece of lettuce, she was in love.

There was something about Charlotte that Jayden was connecting with. Maybe it was the kindness that she experienced when she gently took the food from her hand. Or the unexpected feeling that she was meeting a fellow soulmate. Either way, there was something about her that pulled at Jayden. The two were connected somehow; she could feel it deep within her bones. "She's so beautiful," Jayden said in a soft voice as Charlotte swam over to Sam. She noticed a long scar that ran down the left side of her shell and disfigured her back left flipper.

Jayden's heart saddened. "What happened to her?"

"My guess is it's from a tiger shark, but who knows? The propeller of a boat could have gotten her when she was younger."

Jayden wanted to put her hand on Charlotte's scar, as if doing so would somehow take away whatever pain the animal might still be feeling. She wondered if Charlotte ever relived the nightmare of that moment or if the disfigurement caused her to feel incomplete somehow.

Sam pulled out the last lettuce leaf and handed it to Charlotte. She devoured it in three big bites. "That's it, old girl."

Charlotte stayed with them another fifteen minutes, bobbing and swimming until something else seemed to call her back to the deeper sea. But as she swam away, she raised her head above the water, craned her neck, and locked eyes with Jayden. They stared at the other, neither blinking until Charlotte submerged and disappeared.

As they stumbled out of the water, Jayden couldn't stop thinking about Charlotte. It was the first time she had ever interacted with a wild animal, and although she was trying hard not to anthropomorphize her interaction, she couldn't shake the instinctive feeling that the sea turtle was trying to communicate with her. Or maybe it was the other way around; maybe she was trying to communicate with Charlotte. Trying to somehow let her know she too had been through something traumatic. As though that bonded them in its own way. A sisterhood of sorts, that only the other understood.

"Ouch." Taylor stumbled against her.

Jayden steadied her. "You okay?"

"Yeah, I just stepped on something really sharp." She brushed a top layer of sand away and picked up a white shell covered in spikes. She cocked her arm back as if to throw when Jayden stopped her. The shell, although imperfect, glistened in Taylor's hand. and the polished pink hue of the inside caught her eye. It would make the perfect souvenir to mark the first of what she had hoped would be many more amazing memories with Taylor.

"It's beautiful. Can I have it?"

Taylor turned and handed her the shell. "To my adventurous wife," she said light-heartedly.

"Why thank you, my gracious wife, I shall treasure it forever," Jayden said as she and Taylor giggled their way back to the property. As she veered off and headed for her cottage, she took a good look at the seashell and wondered what type of creature had once inhabited it. Whatever it was, it had left behind a beautiful reminder of a life once lived. She reflected on her own life. What would she leave behind after she was gone? Sadness washed over her when she realized she had no answer to that question.

But then again, she pondered as she shuffled into the cottage and to her bedroom. Maybe leaving behind a memory that elicited a smile when someone remembered her was enough to mark a life once lived. She placed the shell on her nightstand and was thankful she had something to remember the day by. As she peeled off her wet clothes and headed for the shower, she thought about Taylor. She'd seen something in her today that she had never seen during their gym time together. "Happiness." And as the warm water washed away the sand and salt, she thought about herself. She couldn't remember the last time she'd truly felt this happy. As she soaped up her body, her mind drifted back to Taylor, and she shivered. Apparently, the sensation of happiness wasn't the only thing she was feeling.

After showers and snacks, Jayden and Taylor started the tedious process of gathering Frank's WWII memorabilia so they could ship it to a museum in Washington, DC that enthusiastically expressed how much they would love the donations.

"Your grandfather was really obsessed." Jayden placed another painting in the pile accumulating in the middle of the living room.

"Yeah, kinda weird for someone who never saw any action."

"You're kidding me." Wow, for someone who'd never seen battle, he sure seemed to idolize it. "I guess I just assumed he was in the thick of it all based on this stuff."

"Not even close, according to mom. He had a low-ranking administrative job at the base in Pearl Harbor a few years after the war. Besides, Grandpa was a small, skinny guy who wore super thick glasses, so I don't think he would have even been allowed to go into combat."

Jayden laughed at her image. "Holy hell, I guess I just pictured him as some super macho military guy."

"I think deep down, he always wanted to be like that, but in reality, he was just a nerdy little pencil pusher."

"Huh." She glanced around the room. "Well, if he was just a low-ranking admin, how could he afford this house?"

Taylor shrugged. "I asked the lawyer that same question, and he didn't know. But he did say that—"

The rapid honking from a car interrupted Taylor and brought them scurrying to the front porch. Sam was sitting inside a black Ford F-150, his palm pressed firmly against the horn.

"What the hell, Sam?" Taylor yelled as she placed her hands over her ears.

Sam jumped out of the truck and leaned against the hood. "I ran into a buddy of mine at the hardware store. He mentioned he was selling his truck and asked if I knew of anyone who might be interested. We swapped cars for a few hours so I could bring this bad boy back here and show it to you. You said you were in the market for a vehicle, and this one's only three years old."

Taylor bounced off the porch and over to the truck. "Oh yeah, how much?" She opened the driver-side door and hopped in.

"Don't know, but why don't you take it for a test ride and check it out? My buddy said if you like it, he'll make you a good deal."

Taylor adjusted the rearview mirror and seat. "Tell you what." She leaned out the window as Sam pulled shipping supplies out of the bed of the truck and stacked them on the porch. "I'll take it into town and grab us some dinner. If I like the way it feels, I'll see what he wants for it."

As Taylor headed down the driveway Sam handed Jayden a plastic bag containing four rolls of clear packaging tape. "You didn't want to ride with her?" he asked as he grabbed several of the boxes and walked into the house.

"No need, it's her decision." Jayden shrugged.

"Yeah, but you guys are married, shouldn't you at least have a say in it?" Sam dropped the boxes on the floor next to the pile.

"Oh, um, yes well," Jayden stuttered. "She makes all the financial decisions in our marriage, and I, um, make all the decorating decisions." She slightly rolled her eyes at how lame she sounded. And based on the way Sam was looking at her, she was sure his bullshit meter was pinging.

"Oh," Sam mumbled. "I guess that works."

Jayden hated lying to Sam. She liked him, and not telling him the truth about her arrangement with Taylor just didn't feel right. She'd already caught him studying her and Taylor as though he was trying to figure out why she lived in the cottage while Taylor had the master bedroom. Jayden sensed Sam already figured out their marriage was a scam; he just lacked the details.

"Sam, there's something I should tell…" Jayden caught herself midsentence. Was it her place to give up Taylor's secret? No, it wasn't.

"Yeah?" Sam looked up from the box he was assembling.

"Nothing," she mumbled as she shook her head. It should be up to Taylor to let Sam in. It was her story to tell, not Jayden's.

Jayden and Sam wrapped and packed thirteen boxes of Frank's stuff before they heard Taylor return. A minute later, Taylor pulled open the sliding glass door and walked in, hugging a grocery-size paper bag full of food.

"Smells good. Where'd you go?" Sam asked.

"A place called Alfon's Italian Kitchen off South Kihei Road. It got a four-and-a-half-star review," Taylor announced as she walked into the kitchen and placed the bag on the table. "And I got two extra dishes so you can take them home to your grandmother."

"Thanks, Taylor. That was nice of you." Sam smiled.

"As soon as we fix the place up, maybe you can bring her over for dinner one night?" Taylor asked as she began pulling containers out of the bag.

Instead of answering, Sam changed the subject. "So what do you think of the truck?"

"I love it. Tell your friend I'd like to talk to him about buying it."

Sam dug into the side pocket of his cargo shorts, pulled out his cell phone, and fired off a text. A notification chimed within seconds. "He said, let's talk."

Fifteen minutes later, Taylor and Sam's buddy had agreed on a price. By the end of the week, she had the title in hand, her rental Jeep returned, and the gayest B and B in Maui was one step closer to becoming a reality.

In what was becoming her nightly ritual, Jayden strolled down to the beach to snap a picture of the sunset and send it to Andy. A sailboat was rapidly making its way across the water, and she waited until it sailed in front of the setting sun to snap the picture. She fired it off to Andy and captioned it, *First week sailed by. 51 left.* Seconds later, a pouty face emoji appeared, and she couldn't have agreed more. One week in and she had made a new friend in Sam, felt closer to Taylor than she had the entire time they were together at the gym, and she'd connected with a sea turtle. In only seven days, she had managed to do the one thing she promised herself she wouldn't do: get attached.

CHAPTER SEVEN

Sleeping in was no longer what the sleep gods had in mind for Jayden. Something inside her seemed to be aligning with the sunrise, and it was starting to become annoyingly exhausting.

"Fine." Jayden threw off her covers, yawned, and rolled out of bed. She stepped out of her flamingo pajamas and into a pair of baggy workout shorts, a sports bra, and an extra-large Maui T-shirt that Sam had given her. She downed two pain pills and limped her way outside.

She palmed her hair back into a ponytail, and as she walked across the lawn toward the beach, she thought of Taylor. She was sure Taylor would be on her third lap around the entire island by now, her gorgeous, sweaty body glistening in the sun. Jayden's body tingled at the thought.

"Okay," she encouraged herself as she twisted her upper torso around in a halfhearted attempt at stretching. "You've got this." She took two deep breaths, shook out her limbs, then started to jog down the beach. After the first minute elapsed, she had only gained a few yards and was already exhausted. Her feet just couldn't get much traction in the soft sand, and it felt like she was jogging in place. And sure enough, a quick glance to her right confirmed that she was still parallel to the B and B. "I hate running," she wheezed as she leaned forward, put her hands on her knees, and breathed heavily. From the corner of her eye, she watched two runners effortlessly jog along the lower part of the sand, closer to the waves. One turned to her and waved. *Showoff.* She grunted as she smiled and nodded back.

Jayden took the cue from the runners and lumbered down to where the sand was wet and more compact. After another minute of stretching, she started round two of her Maui-a-thon. It was noticeably easier to run on the compact sand, and by easier, her body was actually moving forward. It didn't matter that she was traveling at a speed where a tiny sea crab could have lapped her twice over. She was headed in the right direction, and that was all that counted.

She focused on a boulder about a quarter mile up the beach and decided if she made it to that rock and back, the morning would be a success. Jayden took a deep breath and started to pump her arms, hoping her legs would match the pace. *Why is running so much harder outside than in the gym?* She became convinced the gravity in Hawaii had a different pull because holy hell, moving a body on sand wasn't anything like moving it on a treadmill. But bit by bit, in a walk more than a jog, Jayden finally made it to the boulder.

She reached out and touched the rock for no other reason than to prove she'd made it to her destination. As she turned and began retracing her steps, she decided walking was her best course of action. Even with two pills in her system, Jayden's leg was beginning to throb, and the morning sun was starting to beat down on her. *Note to self, never leave the cottage without a hat and sunglasses.* As Jayden made her way back to the B and B, her body had worked up enough sweat for her to feel like she'd put in a decent workout.

She was hot and sticky, and as she watched the waves lap onto the shore, she found herself gravitating toward the ocean until the water wrapped around her ankles. Five steps later, she was diving under a wave and paddling out far enough to tread water but not far enough to feel uncomfortable. In her mind, there was a fine line between where she was safe in the ocean and where she was shark food.

As she began moving her arms and legs in a slow back and forth rhythm, the throbbing in her leg started to subside. Jayden closed her eyes and wondered again how she got so lucky to live at a B and B in Maui. "Ha." She snorted, surprised by the word that jumped into her head. *Lucky* was definitely a word she had never used to describe her life.

It wasn't like Jayden had a bad life. It was just that she'd never viewed anything that happened in her life as lucky. The word *unfortunate* seemed to fit better, she thought as she continued to tread water at an easy pace. In fact, it was the exact word her ex-girlfriend Carol had kept using in hushed condescending tones during their entire four-year relationship. *Babe, it's not your fault you're heavy, you're just the recipient of unfortunate genes. Babe, the accident wasn't your fault, you were just an unfortunate victim. Babe, I really do love you, but unfortunately, this relationship just isn't working for me.*

Jayden sighed. It was as though her whole existence was one mistake that rolled into another. She'd even overheard her mom tell a friend that her pregnancy was an *unfortunate* lapse in judgment one evening after too much wine during a time in her cycle when she knew better. Jayden closed her eyes and willed the negative thoughts from her mind. She was getting tired of hanging that word around her neck as a warning to all who approached. *Warning, you are about to enter the personal space of an unfortunate soul, proceed with caution.*

Jayden picked up her pace as she worked out her anger in the water. The hurt, rage, depression, and all-around shitty feelings were starting to express themselves with each kick and movement of her arms. Her emotions were turning into adrenaline, and the weightless magic of the water was allowing her to kick and punch it out. Tears welled in her eyes. Damn it, and she'd thought for sure she had put a padlock on the memory door a long time ago. She treaded water faster and faster as the tears flowed from her eyes, blurring her vision. She rubbed her eyes and regretted the move.

"Ow, ow, ow." She closed her eyes and let her tears wash away the newly deposited salt that now felt like tiny needles poking her eyeballs. A minute later, she blinked her bloodshot eyes open as a head popped out of the water a couple of yards away. Jayden's breath caught for a moment as fear gripped her, then she blinked in the familiar face of Charlotte.

Jayden smiled. "Well, good morning." Charlotte swam two circles around Jayden, never taking an eye off her. "I'm sorry, sweetie, I don't have any food right now."

Charlotte bobbed in the surf, cocked her head, and waited for a treat. Jayden held her hands out of the water as if this would convince Charlotte that she was indeed telling the truth, and not in fact lying to her. Charlotte swam so close to her hands, her front flipper hit Jayden's chest. The urge to reach out and pet her surged through Jayden, but caution took over as she focused on Charlotte's beak-like mouth and thought it could do some damage to her fingers if Charlotte wasn't in the mood for a morning head rub. Better to play it safe until they got to know each other better.

Charlotte stuck around for several minutes, until it was clear that breakfast needed to be found elsewhere. She gracefully swam two circles around Jayden, then slowly made her way back to deeper ocean to find some morning munchies. Jayden was sorry to see her leave and waved good-bye to her new aquatic friend.

"She likes you."

Jayden spun and saw Taylor standing on the beach, staring at her. Her breath caught. How long had she been there? An excited twinge tickled its way up her body, and her nipples hardened at the thought of Taylor watching her. "I hadn't planned on being in the ocean this morning or else I would have brought her some food." Jayden stared at Taylor as she paddled to shore. It was obvious Taylor had just finished her morning jog, but unlike Jayden, she probably ran the entire time. "Damn it," Jayden mumbled to herself as she smiled at Taylor; no one had a right to look that good this early in the morning.

"Oh yeah, then how did you end up in the water?"

"Gravity," Jayden huffed as she stumbled out of the water.

"Gravity?" Taylor chuckled as she reached for Jayden's arm and helped steady her.

"Yeah, there's too much of it mixed into the sand, and it was wreaking havoc on my morning jog." Jayden took a second to catch her breath as she turned to Taylor, "I think my first mistake was trying to exercise without my blood laced with caffeine. My second mistake was actually exercising."

Taylor laughed. "Well, it's nice to see you out enjoying the morning." Taylor matched Jayden's stride as they shuffled to the house. "How about you go shower while I put a pot of coffee on for both of us?"

"You have a deal." Jayden turned and headed toward the cottage. "Think Sam will bring us some amazing scones again today?"

"I hope so, but if not, I'll go out and get some."

Jayden nodded as they split off and went their separate ways. Yeah, Jayden thought as she turned the doorknob to her temporary home, *lucky* was definitely the word she would now use to describe her life.

❖

Sam pulled his car to the end of the gravel driveway and scooted out of the driver's side door.

"Hey, Sam." Jayden waved as she walked to the house, feeling refreshed, happy, and hungry.

"Hey, Jayden." He leaned back into his car and retrieved a white bag. "How's your morning so far?" he asked as he walked up to the house with her.

"I went into the water, and Charlotte came right up to me." She beamed. "And oh my God, please tell me those are scones."

"Today's flavor is cranberry walnut." He gave the bag a slight shake.

"You do realize you're going to turn me into an addict."

"They're the best on the island." He stayed behind her as she slowly navigated the porch stairs one at a time. "So Charlotte just came right up to you, huh?"

"Yeah, and swam around me twice hoping I'd feed her, but when she realized I didn't have anything, she just hung out with me for a while before swimming off."

Sam pulled the sliding door open. "She likes you. That's a good sign."

"Then I will graciously thank her with a big 'ol head of lettuce this afternoon."

He smiled. "She'd like that, food always gets Charlotte's attention."

They walked into the kitchen. Taylor had placed three mugs next to a freshly brewed pot of coffee. "Sounds like she's in the shower." Sam tossed the bag of scones on the kitchen table. "Should we wait until she comes out before we have breakfast?"

"Let's wait for her to get out before we dive into the scones but not the coffee." She grabbed the pot and filled a mug for her and Sam. She topped both off with almond milk. "Here's to the start of a wonderful day." She clinked his mug, then took a cautious sip of the hot liquid. Damn, there was nothing like fresh-brewed coffee in the morning. She eyed the bag of scones, and her stomach began to growl. No, she scolded herself as she almost reached for one. *Don't be a total heathen Jayden, wait for Taylor.*

"Too bad Frank isn't still alive." Sam pulled out a chair and sat. "I would have loved to see the expression on his face when Taylor turns this place into a gay B and B."

"I take it you didn't like him much?" Jayden leaned against the counter to put as much space between her and the scones as possible. The delicious smell was starting to make her twitch.

Sam shook his head. "He could be a mean son of a bitch at times, that's for sure."

"So I heard."

They fell into a comfortable silence as they drank their coffee. For a moment, Jayden desperately wanted to blurt out all the details of Frank's will and the horrible way he'd tried to set Taylor up. But like before, she opted to bite her tongue. She'd made a promise to Taylor when they'd agreed to this scheme that she wouldn't tell anyone but Andy. But promises, like lies, could be exhausting to keep.

❖

Sticker shock was the best way to describe how Taylor felt when she received the bid from Sam's friends to renovate the house, but Sam assured her they were giving her a great quote. And in truth, Taylor had no clue what the going construction rate was on the island. *Hell, everything in Hawaii is ridiculously expensive, so why not construction?*

Still, for her own peace of mind, she had a top-rated contractor come out and also bid the job. When he came in ten grand over Sam's friend with a start date two months later, Taylor told Sam to book his buddies.

Construction was scheduled to begin in one week. Taylor went online and placed sell orders on enough of her grandfather's stock to cover the cost of everything they needed to renovate and upgrade the house. She was told the job would take a total of five to six weeks to complete. Taylor was anxious to get it done as soon as possible. She wasn't sure if she could ever look upon the place and not feel the sting of resentment and anger, but transforming it seemed like a good start toward healing those wounds. The place was hers now. This was no longer going to be about Frank.

The evening before construction on the gayest B and B in Maui was to begin, Taylor announced she wanted to have a house cleansing ceremony. She gave Sam money and told him to pick up enough ono fish tacos for the three of them, plus whatever he needed to bring home to his grandmother. "Now, then." She announced as she dashed outside and returned with a yellow-handled sledgehammer. She placed it in the middle of the living room and tossed a pair of clear safety goggles on the coffee table. "As soon as Sam gets back, I want to have a cleansing ceremony."

Twenty minutes later, Sam came bounding into the main room. "What's going on?" he asked as he headed toward the kitchen with the food.

"I was thinking, since the guys are going to start tearing down the walls at six in the morning, we should be the ones to get in the first hits. Kinda like a symbolic cleansing, you know, to clear out all of Frank's bad vibes."

"When you said we were going to have a cleansing ceremony," Jayden chimed in, "I thought you meant we were going to walk around the house burning sage. But I must admit, hitting a wall seems so much more therapeutic."

"Exactly." Taylor adjusted the goggles on her face. She grabbed the sledgehammer, walked over to the wall that separated the entryway and the living room, heaved the hammer back, and swung. The force of the hit caused paneling to shatter and pieces of drywall to crumble.

"Holy shit." Sam laughed.

"You know." Taylor yanked the hammer out and turned. "There's something about putting a hole in Frank's wall that feels so incredibly good. Who's next?" She placed the sledgehammer on the floor, removed the goggles, and held them out. She hoped wherever Frank was, he felt the hatred in her blow. *Take that, you bastard.*

"I'm next," Jayden announced as she rocked off the couch and grabbed the safety goggles. She pulled them over her eyes, gripped the hammer, heaved it over her head, and lost her balance as she stumbled backward. Taylor was behind her in an instant, pressing her body against Jayden's back and grabbing the handle as she steadied the hammer.

"Easy does it." She leaned in and spoke softly. Her stomach muscles twitched, and her nipples hardened. Her body was definitely sending her a signal of its desires. She scolded herself. Jayden was her client turned business partner in this marriage scheme. It would not be fair to cross that line. But as she inhaled the lavender scent that she associated with Jayden and pressed her body more firmly against hers, she knew her desires were rapidly erasing that line. She wanted her, and that urge was overpowering any sense of logic.

"Thanks, I..." Jayden said as she turned her head.

Taylor's breath caught. Jayden's lips were so close, all she had to do was pucker, and Jayden would be hers. They stood frozen for what seemed an eternity, neither making a move toward or away from the other. A flash of something familiar reflected in Jayden's baby blues. It was a look that Taylor knew well. *Desire.* But not the kind of desire that Taylor had seen when she pushed Jayden at the gym. No, this look of desire seemed deep, raw, and hungry. She closed her eyes, tilted her head, and let her cheek softly rub against Jayden's. Goose bumps covered her arms, and a shiver tickled its way up her spine. Her nipples were so hard they almost hurt, and she moaned ever so softly into Jayden's ear.

"Yes," Jayden whispered.

A bolt of energy shot through Taylor's body, and the urge to turn Jayden around, press her against the wall, and kiss her in a deep and passionate way surged through her. Taylor was so wired at that moment, she could sprint a mile and not be winded. She took a deep shaky breath, hoping it would calm her.

"You, um…" Taylor's cheek was still pressed against Jayden's as she nibbled the words down her neck. "You should probably try to swing it using a lower grip." She slowly moved her hand down the handle of the hammer as Jayden's fingers followed closely behind. "That should give you, um, better balance." She widened her stance to try to let some air flow through her running shorts and dry the wetness that continued to accumulate.

"Yeah," Jayden choked out.

Taylor needed to back away and clear her head, but their bodies were like two magnets fused together, and before she knew what came over her, she was softly kissing Jayden's neck.

Jayden's breath caught. They wanted each other, of that Taylor was sure. She could feel the unspoken message Jayden was sending, and as she leaned in, Jayden closed her eyes and parted her lips.

"You need some help over there?" Sam called as he scooted off the couch, apparently oblivious to what was happening.

Taylor jerked back as though an ice-cold bucket of water had been dumped on her. "No thanks, Sam, we're um, we're good," she said as she tried to shake off the sexual trance. "You, um, you should be good to go now," Taylor said in a louder voice for Sam's benefit. "Just put your hands here and give it a go."

"Mm-hmm," Jayden mumbled as she gently placed her hands over Taylor's and squeezed.

Taylor's knees buckled. The desire to pin Jayden against the wall and bury her in kisses resurfaced. "I, um," Taylor whispered as she slowly pulled her hands out from Jayden's. "I guess I'll let you get to it then." She gave Jayden's neck a soft kiss as she slowly stepped back.

Jayden let out a breath. "Yeah…um…okay," she mumbled as she cleared her throat, brought her visibly shaky arms back, and swung the hammer forward. The end result to the wall was a dent so miniscule, it looked as though the paneling had nothing more than a warp in it.

Sam nudged between them. "Okay, my turn, my turn." He displayed the excitement of a child about to go on a ride as he grabbed the hammer and motioned to Jayden to hand over the goggles. After a quick adjustment, he checked to make sure no one was behind him, and in one strong swing, smashed the hammer into the wall. A huge piece of drywall and paneling crumbled to the floor. "Wow, that actually did feel good." He jerked the hammer from the wall. "I'm going again," he announced as he whipped the hammer back and slammed it into the wall with everything he had. "One more." He repeated his actions, then lifted the goggles and observed his handywork. "Sweet."

"If you're double-dipping, then I will too." Taylor wiggled her fingers, and Sam took the goggles off and tossed them to her. She had so much sexual energy still surging through her body, she needed a release. Since going for a run at that moment was not an option, she gripped the hammer, squared off with the wall, and repeatedly smashed the paneling. Over and over again, as fast as she could physically swing the hammer, Taylor went to town on the wall. But as she pulverized the paneling, her mind began shifting to her grandfather. Her sexual frustration faded, and a desire to feel loved surface. It was a feeling she had never felt from Frank, and it was the one thing she'd wanted the most.

She thought of all the times he hadn't been there for her or her mom. All because what—Taylor slammed the hammer in the wall—because he was spending time at this place? Taylor jerked the hammer out of the paneling and repeated the motion. Because his military buddies were more important than his own family? Chunks of the wall tumbled to the floor. The more she swung the hammer, the more she felt the anger release through her body. When she stopped her motion, the rapid beating of her heart pounded in her head. She bent and placed her hands on her knees as she tried to catch her breath. Her ribs were expanding and contracting at a rapid pace, sweat dripped from her face onto the floor, and her muscles bulged from the workout.

After a minute, she straightened and glanced at what was left of the wall. The hammer was wedged between two mangled two-by-fours. She could see the sliding glass doors through a gaping hole, which put a smile on her face.

She wiped her face on her shirt, then turned and slowly shuffled past Sam and Jayden. "I'm hungry. Tacos anyone?"

"I think the wall is officially cleansed," Jayden said as she headed toward the kitchen.

"Yeah," Sam mumbled as he followed.

❖

After stuffing themselves, Sam grabbed the extra bag of food and bid them good night. He told them he would be back early in the morning. Since his buddies were going to arrive by six, he wanted to make sure plenty of scones, scrambled eggs, orange juice, and coffee were ready to consume by the time they arrived.

"Join me for a glass of wine on the porch?" Taylor held up two glasses as she cocked her head toward the sliding glass door.

"I would love to." Jayden followed as anticipation surged through her. Her body returned to its heightened sensation as she thought of Taylor continuing what she'd started.

They plopped down on the lounge chairs and sat in silence for a few minutes, sipping their wine. The air was warm, and the sound of the waves slapping against the shore should have put Jayden in a relaxed mood, but her mind was racing a mile a minute. Should she be the first to bring up the big white elephant that sat between them?

An awkward feeling struck her. Maybe she misinterpreted what she thought she felt from Taylor. No. Jayden replayed the moment in her head. The desire between them was real and had it not been for Sam's interruption, they would have kissed. She took another sip of her wine and finally mustered the courage to address the issue. "So I was wondering about earlier and—"

"I don't think I could ever get tired of this view," Taylor said over her. "Oh, I'm sorry, what were you about to say?"

"I, um, no, yeah, it is stunning, isn't it?" Chicken.

She took another sip of wine as she thought about Taylor's reference to the sunset. Maybe that was Taylor's way of saying she didn't want to talk about it? Maybe that was a hint that they should just drop the subject and not discuss what had almost happened. But it did happen, and the lingering sensation of Taylor's soft lips on her neck was proof. Jayden took a deep breath as her mind continued to overthink and overanalyze. She visualized lowering her body on top of Taylor's and kissing her passionately. She wanted her, and not doing anything about it was driving her nuts. *Just get up and kiss her.* But Jayden knew that wasn't going to happen. Impulse came with a sense of confidence, and she knew her self-esteem wasn't as strong as her self-deprecation. Sadly, she would do as she had always done: bow to the intimidation and fear of rejection. "You know…" She followed Taylor's lead down the safe path. "For a long time, I was scared to death of the water because I almost drowned as a kid."

❖

Taylor exhaled a sigh of relief that they weren't talking about what had almost happened. "You almost drowned?" She really needed time to obsess over and process the feelings she was having. Ugh, why was she so nervous to talk about it? *Because you're scared. Scared because you felt something that you've never felt for anyone, and it's confusing you.* She knew she had always been attracted to Jayden, that was a no-brainer, but was the attraction purely sexual, or was she starting to develop real feelings for her? She took another gulp of wine as she wondered.

"My parents took me to a water park. Mom got up to go into the main building and get us some food, and she left my dad in charge of watching me. This is where the story gets derailed, depending on who you believe. According to my dad, he was busy putting sunscreen on, and one second I was there, the next I was gone. According to my mom, Dad was watching other women and not keeping an eye on me. Either way, I made my way to the water, went in without my arm floats, and sank."

"Arm floats?" Taylor asked as she took a gulp of wine.

"Yeah, you know, those blowup little thingies that slipped on your arms to keep you buoyant. Water wings. Didn't you ever have to wear them?"

Taylor laughed as she shook her head.

"Oh, but of course, shortly after you were born, you were probably setting kiddy breast stroke records," Jayden teased.

If she only knew. Taylor thought about all the times she was picked on as a kid and called scrawny. The embarrassment she'd felt in gym class when everyone laughed at her lack of coordination. Or the disheartening thoughts after trying out for multiple sports teams only to be cut. Her present body was in no way a reflection of the one she was born with.

"Well, then you'll be happy to know I flunked out of guppy swim class."

"How could you possibly flunk out of guppy swim class? Is that even a thing?"

"Apparently, I cried hysterically every time my mom put me in the water, and the instructor finally told her to take me home because I was disrupting the class too much. But at least I got a little blue guppy sticker just for showing up. Which, according to my mom, was all I cared about."

Jayden threw her head back and laughed.

Taylor smiled as she watched Jayden. Funny how she had never noticed the dimple on her left cheek before. But then again, she didn't notice much these days. She'd emotionally checked out after her mom died, felt unloved and ridiculed by her grandfather and personally violated after the mugging. She kept her feelings well-guarded and women at arm's length. She was criticized for being emotionally unavailable, uncaring, and mechanical. She never faulted the women who'd told her that because deep down, they were right. But as she sank farther into her cushion, sipping her wine and getting lost in Jayden's lighthearted laughter, she wondered if for the first time in a long time, she was beginning to feel again.

❖

As Jayden's laughter subsided, she glanced at Taylor. She could sense Taylor was lost in thought, and she wished she knew her well enough to be able to ask what she was thinking without feeling as though she were prying.

"So," Taylor asked as she gestured with her wineglass. "You have to finish the story. Tell me what happened after you almost drowned?"

Jayden took a gulp and shrugged. "A lifeguard, who, unlike my father, was actually paying attention, jumped in and pulled me out."

"Were you traumatized by it?"

"You know, when I think back, I'm not sure if it was the near drowning that traumatized me or the intense fighting that constantly took place between my parents afterward."

"They didn't get along?"

"Oil and water. The only thing they had in common was me. To their credit, they tried to make it work for my sake, but their differences were greater than the desire to be a family. I think my mom actually wanted to make it work, but not my dad." Jayden drifted to memories of childhood days when she would sit in her room crying as she rocked back and forth with her hands mashed over her ears to try to drown out the screaming. And the crazy way she would act out in school because she didn't know how else to channel her pent-up fear and anxiety. And of course, the way it eventually played out in all her relationships.

According to her therapist, she had become attracted to women who resembled and reminded her of her dad. They all had wandering eyes, were verbally abusive, and no matter how hard she tried to gain their love and attention, nothing she did was ever good enough. In the end, none of the women had stayed for the long haul, and all had blamed the breakup on not feeling fulfilled. Ironically, the exact reason her dad gave her mom for wanting a divorce and breaking up the family.

It had taken years for her to understand two things. Some people were just empty souls, and no matter how much of herself she gave, it would never be enough. And if she had to chase love or beg for it, was it really the kind of love worth having?

"I often wonder what it would have been like to have a dad." Taylor broke Jayden's thoughts.

"At least you and your mom had a great relationship."

"We did. She was my best friend in so many ways."

"Then you're luckier than most. I would have taken one functioning, emotionally present parent any day over two dysfunctional ones."

Taylor raised her glass. "To the cliche of always wanting what you think you don't have."

Jayden clinked her glass against Taylor's. "Amen, sister." The alcohol was starting to warm her body and relax her mind. She glanced at Taylor and allowed her butterflies to come out of their cage, stretch their wings, and take a few laps around her stomach. She flashed back to Taylor's body pressed against hers. Never in her wildest dreams did she think a woman like Taylor could be even remotely attracted to someone like her.

Someone like her. She frowned as the words echoed in her mind. Maybe it was time to stop thinking she wasn't worthy of love and affection. She flopped her head back over and watched the last glow of the sun dip under the horizon. She wished Taylor was lying next to her, or better yet, on top of her. Hopefully, she thought as she took another sip, the opportunity for that had not been totally lost. Because *someone like her*, she smiled at her sudden boost of self-esteem, was worth it.

CHAPTER EIGHT

It had been three months since they had begun remodeling the house. As Jayden pulled the sliding glass door open, she again marveled at the transformation. The kitchen and sitting room were now one big great room, the wood paneling was gone, and the walls were painted in subtle shades of earth tones. New furniture replaced the old, beautiful lighting fixtures gave each room a showroom quality, shutters replaced curtains, and most importantly, the entire house screamed gay.

A painting of two women making out on a beach as the surf surrounded their naked bodies was front and center on the great room wall. A watercolor print of rainbow-colored flip-flops lined up on a pier overlooking the ocean and a painting of two men holding each other on a paddleboard graced the other walls. Many more prints, knick-knacks, and statues were tastefully placed around the house. Several rainbow wind socks hung from the porch, and a flock of rainbow-colored plastic flamingos were scattered around the front lawn.

Taylor had hired a small local company to design their website. They'd sent a photographer out to take pictures of both the interior and exterior of the house, and Taylor had worked closely with them to make sure the end result captured her vision. Maui's gayest B and B was now officially open for business.

Taylor had bought space in several online gay and lesbian publications and had asked Jayden to set up and handle the social media side of the business. Taylor had told her that she didn't know anything about social media and had no desire to participate in it. When Jayden had asked why, all Taylor would tell her was that she wanted to keep a low profile. Jayden knew that was a blowoff answer. She didn't know a single person who didn't engage in some way or another with social media. But instead of pushing it, she kept her thoughts to herself as she wondered what the story was behind the excuse.

"We have our first booking," Taylor announced as Jayden walked into the kitchen.

"Woo hoo!" She poured a mug of coffee, and grabbed the container of almond milk.

"It's a..." Taylor stopped midsentence as she looked up from the laptop.

"What?" Jayden turned, leaned against the kitchen counter, and glanced at Taylor as she blew across the top of her mug. Today was the day she had decided to showcase her new look. She'd replaced her baggy T-shirts and equally baggy shorts that had become her daily fashion attire. Instead, she was wearing tightly fitted, powder-blue board shorts, and a long-sleeve surfing shirt that hugged every inch of her upper body. Since Taylor had been focusing all her attention on the house in the past several months, Jayden had decided to focus on herself. And her time spent swimming with Charlotte had resulted in gains that not only came with a new look but a new sense of confidence.

"I'm sorry, what?" Taylor said.

"You were about to say something," Jayden asked as she noticed Taylor check out her body.

"I, uh," Taylor mumbled as she glanced back at her computer. "I, uh..."

"Aloha, ladies." Sam came in holding up the familiar white bag. Taylor and Jayden had become so addicted to the scones from his buddy's store that they'd set up a prepaid monthly account. And since the store was on Sam's way to the B and B, a bag was always prepacked and ready to go by the time Sam swung by in the morning. "Today's flavor is mango and macadamia nut. I was told these are...oh my God." Sam stopped as he looked at Jayden. "You look amazing."

Jayden reached for the bag, "I finally broke down and bought some new clothes yesterday. My other ones were becoming too loose to wear." She coyly smiled when in truth, she had been checking out the transformation of her body for a while. She'd waited until she was down to her post-accident weight before buying new clothes for the big reveal. She was beaming with pride. Not so much of the weight loss but because she finally accomplished the goal she had set for herself over a year ago. And she had done it on her own.

"Well, whatever you're doing, keep it up. You really look fantastic."

"Thanks Sam." Jayden had learned after her first attempt at running on the beach that it just wasn't the right fit for her leg. But the buoyancy of the water was another story. Her body felt agile in the ocean. She could move it in ways she couldn't on land. She no longer felt clumsy or awkward splashing around. And as her body began responding to her time in the water, she cut back on her medication and as of last month, had stopped taking her pain pills. The side-effect of detoxing from the medication was a better sense of clarity, less fatigue, no bloating, and an overall feeling of confidence she hadn't had in years, if ever. She promised herself that when she returned home, she was going to join a gym that had a lap pool. Screw treadmills and weight machines; she was a water girl.

Home. The thought was like a vise tightening around her heart. She tried not to think about the expiration date that came with her marriage license. Or about going home and leaving all this behind. She wished beyond words that Taylor would change her mind and let her stay. But that wasn't the deal. No matter how much she loved being here, it was never meant to be anything more than temporary. The sand in the bottom of her hourglass was piling up, and she had better start accepting that reality.

She sighed as she grabbed three small plates out of the cabinet and scooped out one scone per plate as Sam danced around her, preparing his morning mug of coffee. Yet another ritual she was going to miss.

"We have our first booking," Jayden said as Sam flopped in a chair next to Taylor.

"That's awesome." He yawned as he shoved the end of the scone in his mouth.

"You okay today, Sam?" Taylor leaned back in her chair as she glanced at him. "You look like shit this morning. Were you out partying all night?"

"It's not what you think," Sam mumbled as he chewed. "My grandma wasn't feeling well, so I was at the ER with her until three this morning."

"Oh my God, Sam. Is she all right? Do you need to go back home and be with her?" Jayden said with concern.

"She's fine, just a little, um, she just had, um…" Sam groaned. "Let's just say life wasn't providing her body with a moving experience lately, so the hospital gave her something that would."

Jayden and Taylor busted out laughing.

"Can we not talk about this while I'm eating." Sam frowned as he shoved another piece of pastry in his mouth.

"Yeah, sure." Taylor chuckled. "I'm just glad she'll be okay and sorry you were up all night."

Sam yawned. "Thanks." He grabbed his mug, took a sip, and leaned back in the chair. "So what's up with the booking?"

Taylor turned back to her computer screen as she scrolled. "The booking is…" She frowned. "Huh."

"What? What's huh?" Jayden mumbled as she chewed.

"It's a small wedding party, and they want to rent the entire house." Taylor leaned back in her chair as she glanced at Jayden. "The whole house? For how long?" Jayden asked.

"Five days," Taylor replied.

Jayden remained silent. If Taylor accepted this booking, she would need to move into the cottage with Jayden. If that happened, it would be harder for them to sidestep each other like they had been doing these past few months. She finally broke the silence. "You'll just have to move in with me during that time.

"You sure? Because I can get a room somewhere."

"That's ridiculous, we'll both be fine in the cottage. It's just a few days." Sadness washed over Jayden. Did that one moment make things so awkward between them that they couldn't even cohabitate together? She wasn't about to beg Taylor; if she wanted to get a hotel room for that time, so be it. But deep down, Jayden was hoping this might be the push they both needed to stop avoiding the subject and each other.

As if sensing Sam's eyes on her, Jayden turned toward him. "What?" Sam smiled behind his mug. "Don't mind me."

Taylor sighed. "I, um, I think it's time for a conversation that's long overdue." She twisted in her chair. "Jayden and I aren't really married. I mean, yes, we're *legally* married but not, you know, emotionally married."

"Oh." Sam popped the last bite of scone in his mouth. "I hadn't noticed."

Jayden snorted. "Yeah, right."

Sam smiled. "Yeah, okay, I noticed, but I didn't think it was my place to ask."

Jayden breathed a sigh of relief that the secret was finally out. She considered Sam a good friend, and the longer she kept the charade going, the more she felt like she was somehow betraying their friendship.

Taylor grabbed his coffee mug, refreshed it, and plunked it back down in front of him. As she slowly slid back into her chair, she began telling the tale that led to this chapter of the story.

One hour and two refills later, Sam sat back and shook his head. "Frank really was a bastard."

"Yes, he was, but thanks to Jayden"—Taylor looked over and smiled—"in the end, I'll have the last laugh."

"So you're getting divorced in…" Sam trailed off as he counted on his fingers.

"About seven months, right after I get the deed to the property."

He turned to Jayden. "Then what are you going to do?"

"I go back home. To my old life." But that wasn't totally true. This was her home. She felt it in her bones. She had never connected to a place as much as she had the island. She felt alive here, and she dreaded returning to her old life. She cringed. That wasn't a life; it was an existence. It didn't feed her soul. She was just putting in time. Surviving but not thriving. And the reality of that thought was suffocating.

"Huh," Sam said, seemingly lost in thought.

"What?"

"Nothing, I'll just miss you, that's all."

Jayden leaned into Sam and gave him a hug. She was on the verge of tears. She didn't want to leave. Didn't want to say good-bye to all she loved here. And who she loved. She glanced at Taylor. *Why were the things in her life that made her feel whole and complete always temporary?* Family. Relationships. Health. All temporary. And now for the first time in a long time, she had a sense of belonging that was making her feel complete. She no longer felt like the odd one out. And as she nestled a little deeper into Sam's arms, she couldn't shake the feeling that this truly was where she was meant to be. Taylor, the island, Sam, Charlotte. Her happily ever after was here. Not back in Missouri. She just hoped the pieces would come together before time tore them apart.

❖

Taylor checked her phone for the umpteenth time. She had hired a service to pick up the wedding party and was anxious to hear that everyone was on board and accounted for. She was excited and nervous for their arrival. This was the B and B's first big booking, and she was obsessing over every detail.

Sam had introduced her to a private tour company who would handle their snorkeling, waterfall, helicopter, shopping, and cocktail cruise adventures. And now that the B and B was completely renovated and Taylor had a little more time on her hands, maybe she could finally take advantage of some of the many things the island offered.

"Any word?" Jayden grabbed one of the two suitcase handles as Taylor stepped into the cottage, where she'd be staying for the next few nights.

"Just got a text. They're on their way." Taylor shuffled in and froze as she glanced at the large framed print hanging above the couch. It was a close-up shot of a woman with her eyes closed, head thrown back, and lips parted while another woman kissed the lower part of her neck. "Wow."

"I just bought that. I found it in a poster store in one of the strip malls in town. I thought it was beautiful," Jayden said as she stood by Taylor.

"It sure is," she mumbled as she stared at the print. She flashed back to the night her body was pressed against Jayden's, her lips tickling down Jayden's neck. The lavender scent of Jayden's skin, her breath catching as their fingers wrapped around each other's, and the way she whispered the word *yes*.

Taylor quietly moaned as the visions of that night morphed with the women in the print. She took the place of the woman with her head thrown back in an expression of pure passion. She shivered as she wondered if she could ever be capable of letting herself go to the point of feeling completely exposed with someone. But to have such raw emotion, one had to be vulnerable, and she feared that part of her had been locked away for a long time. She glanced again at the print and thought Jayden should have someone like that...someone who could bring passion to the table, not just sex. Someone who could feel vulnerable in her arms and with her heart. And that someone wasn't Taylor.

"You sure you don't want the bedroom?" Jayden motioned to the other room.

"Oh, um." Taylor shifted her glance off the poster. "No, I'll be fine on the pullout. Besides, this way, you don't have to rearrange any of your stuff."

Jayden nodded. "Well, I've never used the pullout, but for the record, the couch cushions are pretty comfortable on their own."

"Oh yeah?"

"Yeah, I can't tell you how many nights I've fallen asleep while eating popcorn and watching TV."

Taylor wanted to say that she loved popcorn and movie nights but shook the thought out of her head. Nights like that could easily lead to sex, and Taylor didn't want to give Jayden any more mixed messages. Since their encounter with the sledgehammer, she had convinced herself that what had transpired between them was the result of pent-up sexual energy from not being with a woman in years. Purely a sexual urge expressing itself, nothing more.

Taylor's phone chimed, and she pulled it out of her cargo shorts. "They'll be here in five minutes. You want to come with me to greet the guests?"

"You go. I think I'll take a walk on the beach."

"Okay." Taylor was a bit disappointed. Having Jayden by her side as she greeted her first guests would have been a nice way to mark the event. But she couldn't really blame her for not wanting to be there. Tonight marked the start of Taylor's new life and dreams...not Jayden's. "See you later tonight?" She lingered as she glanced at Jayden. Damn, those baby blues were going to get the best of her.

"Yep." Jayden nodded.

"Jayden…" Taylor wanted to tell her how beautiful and sexy she was and that it would be an honor to be by her side. But she changed directions and decided to take the coward's path marked, *safe and nondescript words about your feelings.* "Okay, see you later." Taylor instantly rolled her eyes at herself as she shuffled past Jayden and out the door. *I'm so pathetic.*

❖

"Yep." Jayden stood in the living room and sighed. Everything inside her wanted to run out the door, grab Taylor's hand, and stroll with her to greet the first arrivals at the gayest B and B in Maui. She wanted to stand by the side of her beautiful wife and welcome them. But in doing so, she would be perpetuating the lie, and Jayden didn't want to do that to two women who were about to be married for real.

In fact, Jayden had already decided to distance herself from the wedding festivities as much as possible. It wasn't that she didn't want to share in the ceremony of love; it was more like she was…what exactly was she?

"Jealous." There, she said it. Two women, who couldn't imagine a life without the other, were about to begin their happily ever after here while she was counting down the days until she had to leave. And even though it wasn't *technically* a real divorce because the marriage wasn't *technically* a real marriage, the emotions it was triggering were surprising her. She hadn't calculated on falling in love with Taylor and her new life, and she was scared to death of returning to her old ways and habits.

She grabbed her oversized sunglasses, shoved her phone in the pocket of her shorts, and headed out the door. She needed to put a lot of distance between her and Taylor. Soon enough, they would part company for good, so she had better start getting used to that reality.

She started a slow-paced walk up the beach, hoping it would clear the sadness from her mind. Five minutes into her walk, her phone chimed. She smiled when she saw Andy's name. "How's my favorite best friend?"

"Favorite? I better be your one and only."

Jayden laughed. "You are the only one who will always and forever hold that piece of my heart, and you know it."

"That's what I want to hear. Now tell me the latest Maui gossip."

"Well, the wedding party should be arriving any minute. Taylor is going to greet them, settle them in, and show them around. I, on the other hand, decided to go for a walk on the beach."

"Okay, first of all and always, I'm totally jealous of your life. Secondly, why do you sound so down? What's going on that you're not telling me?"

Jayden sighed. "Oh, I don't know. I guess I just really don't want to see a wedding right now."

Andy paused. "Still counting down to your divorce?"

"Yes." Jayden frowned.

"Honey, you're having a mid-marriage crisis."

"A what?"

"Like a mid-life crisis. You know, inevitable mortality, feelings of intense depression, remorse, high levels of anxiety, and the desire to achieve youthfulness or make drastic changes."

"You had another therapy session, didn't you?"

Andy sighed. "Yes, yes, I just made this about me. I know, I'm shameless. But you know me, I can't help it."

"Sweetie, thirty-six is not old."

Andy gasped in a lighthearted way. "How dare you say that number out loud and conjure up the demon? I'm on the wrong side of staring down forty, and when I was a kid, I thought all forty-year-olds were dinosaurs."

Jayden chuckled. Leave it to Andy to lighten her mood. "Please tell me you're still coming out and that you're not too old to fly now that you've matured to almost *that* age."

"Of course I'm still coming out, and maturity has never had anything to do with me. Don't ever say that word and my name in the same sentence. Besides, just wait till you see me in the blue polo shirt I just bought. I've already worn it for the mirror, and it approves."

"Sounds sexy."

"It is. Now, back to you, what's this wedding really triggering?"

"I don't know, nothing…everything."

"Well, that's a broad net."

"I think I'm falling in love."

"Falling? Honey you *fell* off that cliff months ago."

Jayden frowned. "I know."

"So what are you going to do about it?"

"Nothing to do. I will honor the agreement and promise to not be a crying slob when I leave here."

"You're my best friend, so by proximity, you could never be a slob."

"I just don't know what to do, Andy."

"You enjoy the remainder of your time in paradise with a gorgeous woman and let the universe take care of the rest."

Jayden sighed. "Every time the universe has taken care of me, bad things have happened."

"Not all bad things, sweetie. Look around at your life right now and ask yourself how many people would trade places with you in a heartbeat. Me, for one."

"Maybe my life *right now*, but you know the rest of it hasn't exactly been a picnic."

"Whose life has? Look, all I'm saying is, enjoy it for what it is. The Jayden I know has always found a positive way to spin any situation. So don't waste the next few months pouting. It'll cause wrinkles in places you don't want them. Trust me on that one. Now, go enjoy your beach walk and instead of obsessing over the days until your divorce, obsess over the days until you'll see your fabulous best friend."

"I miss you, you know that?"

Andy made a kiss sound in the phone. "Miss you too, sweetie. Now go be amazing and send more pictures. They're my only source of fantasy right now."

"I doubt that."

"You know me well. Love you…bye."

"Bye," Jayden said as she hit the disconnect button and shoved the phone back into her pocket. She took a deep breath and glanced at the ocean. Andy was right; how could she possibly complain about her life right now? But as she meandered along the beach, kicking at the sand, she knew deep down that something had shifted inside her. And as she had done with her accident, she would look back and always measure this moment in time as her life before Maui and her life afterward. And she knew in her heart that she would never be the same.

An hour later, as she was shuffling back to the cottage, Jayden watched a group of women in animated chatter run for the water. The wedding party had begun their stay, and they were literally making a splash on their first evening. She couldn't help but smile. She remembered the feeling when she first arrived. The beauty of this place woke something inside her that she'd never known was asleep.

She stayed away from the bouncing and bubbly women as she headed up the beach to the lawn.

"Hey, I was just about to go looking for you. How was your walk?" Taylor asked as she headed toward Jayden.

"It was wonderful. How's playing hostess going?"

"Great, as you can see." Taylor nodded to the women. "Everyone's happy and having a great time."

Jayden watched as some of the women played in the surf while others stayed on shore, cameras in hand, capturing the memories. "From the looks of it, I'd say they're having a great time." She turned to regard Taylor. "So why were you about to go looking for me?"

"I wanted to see if you wanted to go into town and grab some—"

"Jayden?" A voice interrupted as a woman came walking toward them. "Is that you?"

Jayden squinted as she focused on a woman in a purple bikini with short blond hair. The voice sounded familiar, but the face... *oh my God.* She froze. She hadn't recognized Carol without her long, flowing, brunette hair. The chopped cut and dye job made her look younger and...sexier. "Carol?"

"Holy shit, Jayden, look at you, you look fantastic," Carol said flirtatiously.

"What are you doing here?" Jayden stared in disbelief. Her stomach tightened as she tensed up. She was so preprogrammed to shift into defense mode with Carol that she barely registered her compliment. *Fantastic? Did Carol actually say something complimentary?* What she would have given to hear a word like that when they were lovers, instead of the routine criticisms and complaints.

"I'm with the wedding party."

"The wedding party? But I don't recognize any of those women from when we were together."

"I joined a hiking club after we broke up and became fast friends with the brides. My God, this is a surprise. What are *you* doing here?"

Without thinking, Jayden reached over and grabbed Taylor's hand, "I'm here with my wife. She, um, she owns the house you're staying in. Taylor, Carol...Carol, Taylor."

"Yes, we met." Carol nodded to Taylor. "I just, um..." Carol stuttered as she looked from Taylor back to Jayden. "Your wife, huh? I um, wow, congratulations. I had no idea."

"Well, it's not like we've been in touch or anything." Jayden didn't hold back on the sarcasm.

"No, no we haven't, I guess that one's on me."

You bet that's on you. A surge of anger hit her like a punch to the gut as she remembered the effort she'd put into trying to maintain a *lovers to friends* relationship with Carol. The pathetic groveling she'd done as she'd reached out through texts and social media until Carol had eventually blocked her from her life.

"Carol, come on in," a woman with the wedding party shouted.

"Well." Carol cocked her head toward the group. "Guess I should get back to my friends. It was, um, wow, you really do look great. Guess I'll, uh, guess I'll see you around."

"Yep, guess so," Jayden said as she released Taylor's hand, twiddled her fingers in a halfhearted wave, then turned and scurried for the cottage.

"Your ex, huh?" Taylor said as she hustled to catch up.

"The one and only."

"Bad breakup?"

"That's an understatement." Jayden stomped into the cottage and started pacing in front of the coffee table. "I can't believe this, of all the people in the world to run into on this island."

"What happened, if you don't mind me asking?"

Jayden let out a heavy sigh and flopped next to her on the couch. "We weren't together long. Just over three years. Two of those were before my accident. Those were the better years, and even then, they weren't all that great." Jayden bounced off the couch and headed toward the kitchen. "Wine?"

"Absolutely."

Jayden popped open a bottle of merlot, hooked her finger through the handles of two pink flamingo coffee mugs, and headed back to the main room. "Sorry, I, uh, need to go shopping for wineglasses." She placed the bottle and mugs on the coffee table.

Taylor smiled. "Are you kidding? These are perfectly you."

Perfectly you. The words caused her to pause. She had been so used to apologizing for who she was, she had forgotten that someone could actually like her for just being...herself. An unexpected warmth washed over her as she sank into the couch. When was she going to stop seeing herself through the eyes of others?

"I met Carol at the party of a mutual friend. She approached me, and we started talking. She was confident, had a quick wit and a smile that reeled me in from the moment her lips parted, and the word hello came out. By the time we were both a little liquored up, she'd asked me on a date. I couldn't believe it." Jayden paused to take a gulp.

"Why not?"

"Because she was gorgeous and accomplished. She could've had anyone at that party, and she asked *me* on a date. The first two years were pretty okay. But with Carol, there's an undertow that's always swirling just under her well-manicured surface. The kind of undertow that'll knock you off your feet and throw you into a black hole if you're not paying attention."

"Which is what happened to you?"

"Yep. Carol's really good at mental manipulation. She has a master's in psychology and knows the right words to implant in your mind. You know, those particular words and phrases someone says to you that make you go, huh, I wonder what she meant by that? And then you revisit those words over and over again in your head, usually late at night when you can't sleep. By morning, you're questioning everything you ever thought about yourself and replacing it with what the other person thinks about you." She cringed. It was exactly what she had been doing since the moment she had met Taylor and especially since their intimate embrace. She saw herself as she thought Taylor saw her, letting her own self-doubts steer the internal dialogue and justify the avoidance.

"I think that's called a mind fuck." Taylor took another drink of wine as she relaxed into the cushions.

Jayden nodded. "Yes, it is, and there are those who walk among us who are really good at it. And with Carol, my mind was getting more of a fucking than my body."

Taylor choked and had to lean forward as she coughed.

"Sorry, didn't mean to be crude."

"I'm good with crude." Taylor tapped her fist against her chest as she coughed once more.

"Carol thought I was subpar in a lot of categories. She would ridicule me around friends if I used the wrong words or dressed unbecomingly." Jayden displayed a one-handed air quote. "I was not the woman she thought she should have on her arm, and she made horrible raised eyebrow comments at me when I started to gain weight."

"Why did you stay with this woman?"

"There were moments where she could be really fun and charming and, um, you know…"

"The sex was good."

Jayden sighed. "It'll get you every time. Good sex has a way of shutting down all common sense."

"Yes, yes it does." Taylor took another sip. "So how did it end?"

"After the accident, I was in pretty bad shape. I was laid up for months. I struggled with the physical therapy, and I was in constant pain. Depression set in, and as I became more and more dependent on her, I found out real fast that Carol lacked the caregiving gene. One night, when I was hurting and feeling sorry for myself, she stood from the couch, turned to me, and dramatically announced that this wasn't what she'd signed up for in a relationship. The next day, she left."

"Wow, that was cold."

"Yeah, that's Carol. Fortunately for me, Andy was looking for a place to live because his boyfriend had dumped him for a male model. And, I'm happy to report, Andy is not lacking the caregiving gene at all. In fact, just the opposite. He brought me back from a dark place, and well, now look at me. Drinking wine from a flamingo mug in a beach cottage in Maui." *With a beautiful woman by my side.*

"Well." Taylor said as she grabbed the bottle off the coffee table and topped off her mug. "Carol is a fool."

"I have many more colorful words that better describe her if ever you want to borrow them."

"I bet you do." Taylor laughed as she leaned back into the cushion and flopped her head toward Jayden. "I'm sorry that happened to you."

Jayden waved her hand in dismissal. "Thanks, but Carol leaving me was the best gift she ever gave me. It just took me a while to realize it."

"You going to be okay with her on the property for the next several days?"

"Yeah, I'll be fine. Hopefully, she'll be so busy with the wedding party, we won't see much of each other."

Taylor nodded.

"Um, and thanks again for playing along when I grabbed your hand. I'm sorry if that made you uncomfortable."

"It didn't, and I'm glad I could help."

Jayden tossed her head back and emptied her mug. *Thank God for wine.* A slight numbness was taking hold as she poured herself more. She glanced at Taylor, and a twinge of hope shot through her. She looked so relaxed and comfortable on the couch. *At home*, was the phrase that came to her mind. *Wouldn't it be nice if we really did live together?* "How about popcorn and a rom-com or murder mystery?"

"Are those my only movie choices?"

"Yep, I've already taken the liberty of narrowing them down for you. And you're welcome."

Taylor laughed. "Um, well then, let's do rom-com tonight and murder mystery tomorrow."

"Planning ahead, I like your style. Do you need to check in with the wedding party at all?" As the wine settled in and calmed the last of her agitation, she thought about the wedding party. Everyone seemed so happy. And why not? They were on a beautiful island and were about to participate in a ceremony of love. *Love.* She twirled her wedding ring, glanced at Taylor, and let out a frustrated sigh. Why was love so hard to find and so much harder to hold on to?

"Nope, the house is theirs. If they need anything, they know where to find me, plus I gave them mine and Sam's cell numbers so they can shoot us a text if something major happens."

"Then I say, we both relax. You've put in a lot of hours prepping the house for them, as opposed to me, who hasn't helped much at all."

"Hey, you pitched in plenty."

"Nowhere close, but I'm never one to turn down a compliment." Jayden raised her mug and took another drink. "What time tomorrow are you setting up for the reception?"

"The wedding party booked a reservation for the Haleakala Crater sunrise tour and a brunch afterward, so while they're doing that, Sam and I will set up."

"Holy shit, on their wedding day they booked a sunrise tour?"

"They said they wanted a sunrise shot to go along with the wedding's sunset shot. The photographer is meeting them here at four in the morning and basically hanging with them the entire day to capture everything."

"Sounds so romantic, but they're going to be fried." Jayden went into the kitchen and pulled the air popper down from the cabinet. She thought back to her wedding day with Taylor. Not at all a picture-book wedding, not even close. The fact that no one had thought about snapping one single photo of the ceremony was an indication of how unromantic everyone had thought the event was. Oh well. She shrugged. Hopefully, she could make up for it at her next wedding…if she was lucky enough to have one.

❖

"I know, but what a wonderful day they'll have." It bothered Taylor when she thought about the fact that neither she nor Annie had taken any pictures of her wedding with Jayden. At the time, it hadn't seemed important. Why mark a day that was nothing more than a business arrangement? But lately, Taylor wished she had a few photos in her phone that she could scroll back to. She smiled at the memory of Jayden placing the ring on her finger, looking all bashful and beautiful, and wished she had frozen that moment in time.

"Want melted butter on top?" Jayden called.

"Yes, please. I think this night calls for decadence."

"If you think melted butter is decadent, I hate to tell you this, but you need to expand your horizons. There's a whole lot of decadence out there that makes melted butter look pretty pathetic."

Taylor chuckled. "You know, for the longest time, I deprived myself of stuff like that so I could maintain my body." She thought of her early days at the gym. She was so hyper focused on turning her body into a finely tuned machine that she'd refused to allow herself anything that would slow her gains or compromise the progress. She ate clean foods, cut out the alcohol, and sacrificed a lot of life's pleasures. It wasn't until a few years ago, during a birthday celebration for Annie, that she'd finally loosened up. And now, as she comfortably sat with Jayden, she was thankful that she could share moments like this in all its decadent glory and not be so hung up on the other crap.

"While I, on the other hand, worked hard to maintain my taste buds," Jayden said with a smirk. "You pick the movie while

I make noise in here." She popped two big bowls of popcorn and walked them into the living room, placing one in front of Taylor and the other in front of her seat.

"I just noticed, you're hardly limping at all." First the weight loss and now the limp. Ugh. Taylor scolded herself and wondered what other transformations she'd missed in Jayden because she'd been so preoccupied with the renovations.

"Yeah, I don't know if it's the warm weather, the loss of weight, or the swimming, but my leg feels the best it ever has. Well, I mean, since the accident. And I'm completely off the pain pills."

"Jayden, that's wonderful."

Jayden dug her hand in the popcorn and shoved a few pieces in her mouth. "Thanks. I have to say, it really feels good not being on those pills. The side-effects weren't too nice, and besides, I couldn't drink alcohol, although every now and then, I did indulge. I seem to have an aversion to certain rules. At least, that's what my mother used to tell me."

"I bet you were an adorable kid." Taylor grabbed the salt shaker from the kitchen.

"Adorable was never used by my parents in their string of words to describe me."

"I find that hard to believe." She regarded Jayden as she sprinkled more salt in her bowl. She couldn't attest to what Jayden had been like as a child, but the woman sitting next to her was sweet, charming, and beautiful. "Ready for a rom-com?"

"Did you pick a good one?"

"I think so. It got five out of five stars, and the actress looks sexy as hell."

"Then you have done your job well. Fire up the movie."

She hit the remote and thought about the nights she and Annie had watched movies together. She was comfortable and relaxed with Annie in ways she never felt from a lover. And right now, as she nestled into the couch next to Jayden, those same feelings returned. She was content in this moment, and it felt nice. She cleared her mind of its typical jumble of random thoughts and tried not to obsess over anything. The wedding party was fine, the house looked amazing, and she was enjoying Jayden's company. Life was good.

❖

Jayden wiped away a tear as the credits rolled. "That was so romantic. Predictable as hell but totally romantic." She didn't care that the story was a bit farfetched and unrealistic. What mattered was love conquered all, and that thought alone was what always kept her optimistic that one day, her own love story would have the same romantic ending.

"It's been a while since I've watched one of these movies."

"*These* movies? I'll have you know *these* movies got me through some pretty serious heartaches."

"Oh yeah, how many women have you been with, if you don't mind me asking?"

"Before I answer that question, is there a number you have in mind that would lower your opinion of me?"

Taylor chuckled. "No, of course not."

"One-night stands included?"

"Um, sure."

Jayden mentally counted. "Well, then, the magic number is lucky thirteen." She cringed. Had she really been with that many women? Was thirteen even considered *that* many? She cautiously focused on Taylor's face to see if her expression gave a hint as to what she was thinking.

Taylor nodded. "Thirteen, huh?"

"Yeah, but only two that mattered."

"Carol being one of them?"

"Yes." Jayden nodded. "What about you?"

"Including one-night stands, about fifteen."

"And of those, how many really mattered?"

Taylor fidgeted a few seconds before answering. "None."

"What? None?" Wow, was she kidding? How was that even possible? For Taylor to never find a love that really mattered saddened Jayden. Granted, she had only fallen for two women, but at least she could say she loved them enough to feel the sting of heartache. She knew what it was like to lose something she wanted to hold on to. Even if the relationship was short-lived and dysfunctional, she could still look back and say there had been someone in her life who at one time really mattered to her. But none?

"I guess I just haven't met the right one yet."

"But you've been in a long-term relationship, right?" Her heart was hurting for Taylor. What had happened in her life that prevented her from finding a love that mattered?

"Three, and not the longest of terms." Taylor rubbed the back of her neck. "There was always one of us who didn't feel complete." Taylor paused, then softly mumbled, "At least, that's what they always told me."

Jayden regarded her. Interesting word. Could she honestly say any of her relationships had been complete? Was there even such a thing? "Wow, I totally get that. In fact, I could kinda say the same about my relationships. I mean, don't get me wrong, I think I was in love for a little while, but looking back, there was always something that was off."

"Like there's a part of you that you can't completely share because you don't feel settled within yourself enough to totally open up to your lover?"

Jayden regarded Taylor. That wasn't what she was alluding to at all. In fact, for her, it was just the opposite. She was the one who was an open book in a relationship, and her girlfriends were the ones who were more withdrawn. Hmm. Was she repeating a pattern with Taylor? Was she wanting something from her that she was incapable of giving? "More like I seem to have a habit of picking people who are a bit whack-a-do."

Taylor laughed as she stood and grabbed the empty bowls. "Whack-a-do?"

"Yeah, you know, one step away from being completely erratic."

Taylor placed the bowls in the sink. "I know all about that. Can I get you anything else from the kitchen?"

"How are your hot chocolate making skills?"

"Michelin-star worthy."

"Good because I picked up some at the store the other day, and I'm kinda craving a cup right now. There's even extra chocolate in the pantry above the coffee machine. You know, just throwing it out there in case your Michelin-star recipe calls for it."

"Extra chocolate it is." Taylor smiled as she moved around the kitchen.

As she watched Taylor make herself at home, Jayden couldn't help wonder what it would be like to be married to her for real. To have a ritual between them that was comfortable and easy. To go about their lives connected yet independent. Nothing forced, nothing fake, and no secrets. Yeah, Jayden thought as she watched Taylor pull two mugs down from the cabinet, life with Taylor was something she could easily wrap her head around. She just wished she could do the same with the rest of her body.

CHAPTER NINE

Jayden woke to the sound of Sam and Taylor talking outside the cottage. She rolled out of bed and shuffled into the main room. The couch was put back together, and in the kitchen, a fresh pot of coffee was waiting for her. She grabbed the pot and filled her mug. Yeah, she thought as she blew across the hot liquid, married life was definitely something she could get used to.

She headed out the door and across the lawn. Sam was giving Taylor another history lesson on the island as they set up the long buffet table. Having only six people in the wedding party made setting up for the ceremony super easy to do. Since the brides wanted to be married on the beach right at sunset, there were no frills and no extra requests. Just them, the beach, and a perfect setting sun.

"What can I do to help?" Jayden came up behind Taylor, who was throwing a linen tablecloth over the banquet table. How was it that no matter what time of the day it was, or what Taylor was doing, she always looked beautiful?

Taylor turned and smiled. "I hope we didn't wake you. We were trying to be as quiet as possible."

"You should have gotten me up when you got up, and I could have pitched in from the start." She was keenly aware that Taylor had given her all the nonphysical tasks to do during the renovation. But her recent physical gains had come with a renewed sense of confidence, and she was anxious to finally start pitching in with the physical tasks as well.

Taylor shook her head. "No need, we easily have it covered. Finish your coffee, go enjoy your morning with Charlotte, and when you get back, let's have breakfast. Today's scone is strawberry and mango."

"That sounds amazing."

"They are," Sam chimed in as he rolled the round table in place and kicked at its legs.

"You sure I can't help?" She said with a twinge of guilt.

Again, Taylor shook her head. "It's an easy morning, go enjoy your swim."

Yeah, Jayden thought as she turned and headed back to the cottage, I definitely could get used to this. She finished her coffee and threw on a pair of flamingo boardshorts and a sports bra. She grabbed a huge handful of lettuce from the refrigerator and headed to the water. By the time she was waist deep, a familiar head popped up and greeted her.

"Hello, Charlotte, how are you this morning?"

Charlotte gave Jayden her fixed reptilian stare as she gently nibbled a lettuce leaf. She might not have had the facial muscles that other animals used to express their emotions, but Jayden was convinced she understood Charlotte well enough to read her thoughts. To Jayden, Charlotte's head bobs, blinks, and the tiny bubbles she blew from her nose all conveyed a specific emotion.

"Here's the daily news brief: turns out my ex is a part of the wedding party, so she's staying at the house for the next several days. Let me tell you what a shock that was. I haven't seen or talked to her in years, and bang, she just pops back into my life. And all of those horrible feelings I had about myself when we were together resurfaced. I guess I was just fooling myself when I thought I was totally healed from that relationship. But I guess you're never totally healed from something that hurt you so much, huh, girl?" She pulled out another leaf. "Anyway, I'll have to point her out to you so if you see her in the water, you can bite her toe or something. No, don't, but it is a fun thought."

Jayden watched Charlotte bob in the waves and chomp on the lettuce. "On another note, and I know you know this, but I finally admitted to myself that I'm in love with Taylor. I know, right? That's what I thought too. Last night, we were watching TV and eating popcorn and drinking hot chocolate, and it all just felt so right." Jayden handed Charlotte more lettuce as she tilted her head slightly and blinked. "My thoughts exactly." Jayden smiled. "And just between us, well, and Andy too, but since he's not here right now, I'll tell you. I wish my marriage was for real, and I could stay here forever."

Charlotte blinked again as Jayden handed off the last of the produce. If what she read about the myths of sea turtles was right and they really were guardian spirits and animals that brought good luck, then maybe hanging out with Charlotte would make her wish come true. Wouldn't that be nice?

As Charlotte finished her breakfast, Jayden began her morning exercise routine of treading water mixed with moves she'd borrowed from a video she'd watched on water aerobics. She loved everything about her life right now, and she was starting to become depressed that it would soon come to an end. Oh well, the universe had never been completely kind to her, so why start now? But damn it, how nice it would be to finally catch a break. "Take a number," she whispered to herself as Charlotte swam around her in their usual morning routine. "Everyone has it rough," Jayden mumbled as Charlotte's scar caught her eye. For such a peaceful soul, a lot of things seemed like they were out to get her. Between sharks, fishing nets, boats, and pollution, Charlotte's future seemed a hell of a lot more questionable than Jayden's. And yet, from what Jayden saw, Charlotte never seemed to have a bad day.

As Jayden finished the last of her workout, Charlotte swam two circles around her and headed out into the deep blue. "Stay safe, old girl, see you tomorrow."

❖

The wedding group returned from the crater at around two in the afternoon. Taylor didn't know if they all took naps or continued with the festivities, but everyone looked refreshed and beautiful as they stepped out from the house that evening and gathered on the lawn. One bride opted for casual cotton slacks and a dress shirt, while the other wore a beautiful white sundress. Both looked happy and in love. She felt a ping of jealousy, then decided that no, it wasn't jealousy she was feeling. It was more like curiosity. She'd never had a healthy relationship as a role model when she was growing up. What was it like when two people loved each other so much they decided all the work and drama of a relationship was worth it? That one couldn't imagine a world without the other in it? She had only seen it play out in rom-coms like the one she'd watched last night with Jayden. But that was fantasy. Scripted words and directed scenes. But as she watched the women kiss, she wondered, could love really be all that really mattered in the end?

The caterers were set and ready to serve on cue, and Sam had sprinkled Singapore plumeria flowers over the lawn, giving the property an almost fairytale look. The brides had hired a local Hawaiian preacher, who was signaling to everyone that it was time to head to the ocean. The sunset was nearing its golden glow, and Taylor knew the pictures would be spectacular. And as she watched the group follow the preacher like baby ducks to the beach, she again wished she would have had Annie take a few pictures of her and Jayden. Fake wedding or not, the moment should have been captured, not dismissed. She blamed herself for that. She was so focused on the business side of the arrangement, she'd forgotten about the emotional side of it.

She sighed as she looked for Jayden. "You know, if I can see you peeking through the bushes, chances are, so can everyone else."

"Jeezus!" Jayden jumped, and the limb from the hibiscus bush she was holding swung back and slapped her in the face. "Ouch." She rubbed her forehead.

"Oh my God, are you okay?" Taylor held back the urge to close the distance between them and gently kiss the red spot forming on Jayden's forehead and make it better. *God, she was so adorable.*

Jayden nodded. "Guess I deserved that, and um, this isn't what it looks like. Well, maybe a little."

"Come on, Peeping Tom," Taylor smiled. "Whaddya say we sit in front of the cottage like normal people and have some wine?"

Jayden stopped rubbing her forehead and grinned. "Best invitation of the day."

"Good." Taylor dashed into the cottage. "I was hoping you'd say yes." She said as she emerged with a bottle of wine in one hand and two flamingo mugs in the other.

Jayden sat in one of the two chairs framing a small table in front of the cottage. "What do you think about the wedding so far?" she asked as Taylor leaned forward in her seat and uncorked the bottle.

She knew which wedding Jayden was referencing, but she still kept flashing back to theirs. Why was she so bothered by it now? They'd both agreed to the terms of their ceremony. Right? But she knew that wasn't true. Jayden agreed to *her* terms. Not theirs. And as she watched Jayden crane her neck toward the ocean, a twinge of guilt punched at her gut. Jayden had deserved a wedding that rivaled her beloved rom-coms. Like the one taking place on the beach right now. Not the one she'd gotten.

"I think it's going great." She tried to shake the thoughts from her mind. She felt like she owed Jayden an apology. "The sunset is perfect, and the caterer is set and ready to serve. If they need anything, they know where to find me." She poured some wine in each mug and handed one to Jayden. "Cheers."

"What are we cheering to?"

Taylor thought for a moment. "How about to a successful first booking for Maui's gayest B and B?"

Jayden clinked Taylor's mug. "And to the amazing woman who made it all happen."

"Well, I couldn't have done it without you."

Jayden snorted, "I beg to differ, considering I haven't done much of anything but tag along."

"That's not true. You married me. Without you, I would have never been handed the keys to this place. So *I* beg to differ." Taylor smiled as Jayden's cheeks flushed. There really was something special about her that Taylor found mesmerizing. She was not like any of the women she had ever been attracted to, and that felt refreshing. But could she really allow herself to feel vulnerable with Jayden in the ways that mattered? She tried to dissect the urges that were rushing through her body as she took another sip. Was this desire purely sexual? Or could this be more? She decided it was time to find out as she slowly leaned across the table and licked her lips in anticipation. She became hyper-focused on every detail in Jayden's face, every muscle twitch and every breath as she came closer…closer. As the tips of their lips touched, a sudden scream made both turn toward the lawn.

One bride scooped up the other and swung her in a circle as the group made their way back from the beach and to the food. Laughter, lighthearted chatter, and love filled the air as Taylor smiled. *Maybe there is such a thing as happily ever after.* "They seem happy." She glanced at Jayden as she took a breath to steady her butterflies. She was amped up and turned on, and she had waited long enough.

"They do." Jayden grabbed the bottle. "More wine?"

"Well, actually." Taylor leaned in to finish what she started.

Someone cleared their throat as Taylor pressed her lips against Jayden's. They again turned away from each other and focused on the figure standing over them. Taylor sighed to herself. "Now what?"

"Sorry to bother you," The caterer said in an apologetic voice. "My bartender isn't feeling well, so I told her to lie down in the van for a few minutes. I can take her place, but that means I'll need help with the catering, and you said—"

Taylor stood. "To come get me if you needed anything." She turned to Jayden. "Please hold that thought, I'll be right back." *And when I do return, I'm going to kiss you deep and never come up for air.*

❖

"Yep, no worries, duty calls." Jayden sighed. Her body was aching to be touched. Her nipples were hard, she was wet, and she had been robbed, yet again, of something she desperately desired. "So close," she mumbled as she took a drink. So damn close.

An hour later, as Jayden was reading the latest breaking news on her phone, Taylor came strolling up and placed two full plates of food on the table.

"Well, that sure took longer than I thought." Taylor handed her a plastic fork and knife, then sat.

"I was just on the verge of feeling totally rejected, but since you come bearing gifts, I shall forgive you." Jayden leaned over the plate. "This looks delicious."

"It is." Taylor smiled. "Hope you're hungry."

"Starving, actually," Jayden shoveled a forkful of stringy cheese lasagna in her mouth. "How's it going out there?"

"Great, the caterer's assistant is feeling better, and everyone's having a good time. But I can tell they're starting to get tired. It's been a long day for them."

"Yes, it has."

"So, um…" Taylor mumbled as she chewed. "I noticed your ex glancing over at you several times this evening. I think she was thinking about asking you to dance."

"What?" Jayden's stomach bottomed out. Dance? With Carol? The last time that happened, she was told she looked so ridiculous she was embarrassing to be around. The last thing in the world she wanted to do was relive that memory. "Why would you think that?"

"Because I caught her staring at you a few times when the slower songs played."

Jayden snorted. "Watch out for Carol's stare. She's Medusa's twin sister, you know."

"Is she?"

Jayden nodded. "She'll turn your self-esteem to stone, then shatter it into a million pieces." Jayden made a bomb dropping noise, followed by an explosion. Funny how quickly she'd lost herself in that relationship, and how long it'd taken to find herself again. But then again, she could argue that she still hadn't completely found herself. *Is anything that's glued back together really as perfect as it once was before it was scattered?*

"Ah, well, then, I'll make sure I never look her in the eyes."

"Smart woman." Jayden stood and arched her back. She grabbed her empty mug, plate of food, and the bottle of wine. "Wanna take this party inside, and maybe…"

Taylor jumped up so quickly, she almost knocked the chair over. She leaned into Jayden's ear. "Finish what we almost started?" she whispered as she nibbled on Jayden's neck.

Okay, holy hell, the temperature just dropped twenty degrees because the chill that shot up Jayden's body caused her to shiver. She hurried into the cottage, and piled everything on the coffee table. As she turned around, she bumped into Taylor. She stumbled backward, but Taylor reached around her waist and pulled her close. She stood frozen for a moment, then slowly leaned in and kissed her.

When their lips first touched, it was soft and gentle. An exploratory peck, but within seconds, a heat ignited within Jayden, and her tongue dove deep, sparking a desire she hadn't felt in a long time. She was breathing heavy as she began to explore Taylor's body.

Taylor finally broke the embrace and leaned into Jayden's ear. "Bedroom."

It wasn't a question; it was a summons, and Jayden gladly obeyed as she grabbed Taylor's hand and led her into the other room. They stood at the side of the bed, and she turned to Taylor, placed her hands on the bottom seam of her T-shirt, and pulled the fabric over her head. "You okay with this?" She didn't wait for an answer as she placed a finger on Taylor's stomach and slowly tickled up each twitching muscle until she hooked the elastic of Taylor's sports bra. A hunger stirred inside her as an urgency to have her desires satisfied took hold.

"Mm-hmm." Taylor nodded as Jayden's breathing accelerated. She lifted the bra over Taylor's nipples. They were hard, and she leaned in and gently sucked on one. As Taylor's moans filled her head and became more intoxicating to her, she pulled the bra off. As she licked her way to the other nipple, she yanked Taylor's shorts down her legs.

She circled her tongue around Taylor's nipple one more time, then leaned back. She wanted to look at Taylor's body, sear the image of every inch of her nakedness into her mind. *Damn she's beautiful.* She cupped Taylor's breasts and moved her thumbs over her still wet nipples. "I'm sorry," Jayden jerked her hands away when Taylor shivered. "Are my hands cold?"

Taylor gently placed Jayden's hands back on her breasts. "Cold hands are not what my body is reacting to."

"I see." Jayden grinned as she leaned in and demanded another tongue-locking kiss.

Taylor moaned as she slowly lowered Jayden to the bed. "I think you need to get naked too, I mean, it's only fair," she said as she remained standing at the side of the bed. Jayden smiled. She wasn't about to relinquish control that fast. If Taylor wanted to take her, then she would have to wait until it was on her terms.

"Oh, I see," Jayden wiggled out of her shirt. "You think I should join you in blissful nakedness, huh?" She unclasped her bra, flung it to the floor, then slowly unzipped her shorts as she glanced at Taylor. She could see the lust in her eyes, and although she'd never thought of herself as an exhibitionist in any way, right now, the act of stripping for Taylor was an unbelievable turn-on.

"Yes, as a matter of fact, I do want you to join me in blissful nakedness. It's a prerequisite for what I have in mind for tonight."

"Well, then." Jayden pushed her shorts to her ankles, took one leg out, then with her other leg, gave a kick, sending her shorts sailing across the room. They came to rest on the beak of the flamingo statue that sat on her dresser. She was enjoying watching Taylor watch her. "I wouldn't want to disappoint."

"Oh, you won't disappoint." Taylor climbed into bed and straddled her. Her biceps bulged as she hovered over Jayden's body, then slowly stretched her legs out as she lowered her hips. When their skin touched, Taylor gently applied the right amount of pressure. Jayden moaned. There was something about feeling another woman on top of her that was such a goddamn turn-on.

"You good?" Taylor gently began grinding.

"Mm-hmm," was all Jayden could say as her eyes rolled back in her head.

Taylor leaned in and sucked on Jayden's neck, then slowly, ever so slowly, licked her way down to Jayden's breast. Her nipples were aching to be touched. Taylor lightly circled and teased the tip of each nipple with her tongue, then settled on the one and started sucking.

"Yes…yes," Jayden whispered as she pressed her hips into Taylor's stomach. She needed more pressure down there, and she needed it now. She moaned again and hoped Taylor understood the signal.

She felt Taylor's fingers playfully linger in her wetness before they entered her. She closed her eyes and arched her back, and as Taylor's fingers picked up their pace, she moved her hips to the rhythm.

"Harder. Faster," she whispered.

"I need a different angle." Taylor slowly slid her fingers out, reached under Jayden's back and gently turned her onto her stomach. The shift in position heightened Jayden's arousal as her mind raced with thoughts of what Taylor was about to do to her. A moment later, she felt Taylor's warm sweaty body press against her back, and Taylor's arms wrapped around hers until their fingers interlocked. Jayden squeezed Taylor's hand. She moved it to her mouth and kissed and licked her fingers. She hoped Taylor was getting off on this as much as she was. A nibble to her neck brought Taylor's soft words to her ears, "I want you."

"Then take me," she breathed through accelerated breath. Taylor slid an arm under Jayden's stomach and coaxed her up onto all fours. She held her in what felt like a strong, yet protective embrace as her wet fingers tickled their way down Jayden's back and made her shiver. She knew where those fingers were headed. A moment later, they once again found her wetness. Jayden's muscles tightened as she felt the fingers massage around her clit. She leaned back into Taylor, hoping to coax her fingers in. But apparently, Taylor wasn't done playing. Jayden lowered her head and arched her back. She was so excited, she could feel herself starting to come. She tensed her muscles and tried to hold back the climax. She wanted Taylor in her when she came. Wanted her to feel her pulsing. Wanted her to...

"Fingers. Now." Jayden exhaled as the sensation of two fingers entering her sent a surge through her body. She felt Taylor release her grip around her stomach and move her hand to the outside of Jayden's clit.

The added pressure outside combined with the thrusting inside caused her muscles to tighten. She clutched at the sheets as she rocked back and forth. The release in her throat came with the same intensity as her orgasm. *Holy hell.* She began to relax her muscles as she felt soft kisses on her back, and her throbbing subsided.

"You're so beautiful." Taylor whispered as she turned Jayden over and collapsed next to her. Both were breathing heavy. They lay side by side until their heart rates and bodies calmed enough for speech to return.

"That...was amazing," Jayden turned and gave Taylor a kiss.

They stayed motionless for another fifteen minutes, not saying much until Jayden leaned on her elbow and gently let her fingers glide over Taylor's body. As she watched Taylor's muscles flinch and twitch under her touch, her desire to take her intensified. She was about to make love to the most beautiful person she knew, and she wanted to treasure every moment.

"You keep that up," Taylor moaned, "and you'll have to finish what you're starting."

"That, my dear, is the plan." She kissed Taylor with renewed hunger. The formalities between them were no longer needed, the subtle asks of, *is this okay,* were gone. Jayden now knew how Taylor played in bed. Now it was her turn to give back everything and more that Taylor had given to her.

CHAPTER TEN

The ear-piercing scream jolted Jayden awake, and her brain tried to understand what it was.

"Did you hear that?" Taylor mumbled in a raspy voice.

"I did," she replied as the second scream had them bolting out of bed and scrambling to find their clothes. Fear gripped her as she thought about the wedding party. Shit. Something bad happened. She ran behind Taylor to the beach. There, Carol stood surrounded by her friends, dripping wet and hysterical.

"What happened?" She pushed her way through the women and placed a protective arm around Carol. She might not like, her but the thought of something bad happening to her was gut-wrenching.

Carol leaned away from Jayden and pointed to the water. "It was about to attack me."

"Oh my God, a shark was about to attack you?" one of the brides said with concern.

Carol shook her head. "No, not a shark, a big—"

"There it is," another bridesmaid called as she pointed to the water. "A shark!"

All eyes were on the ocean as Charlotte bobbed in the surf, her head above the water. Jayden doubled over with laughter, her fear turning into relief in what probably seemed like an inappropriate release of emotion.

"What?" Carol turned to Jayden. "What's so funny? That thing was about to attack me."

Jayden flashed back to her own terror when she first saw Charlotte. She couldn't fault Carol's reaction, but she would never tell her that. "That's not a shark, that's Charlotte. She's a sea turtle, and she's super friendly." Jayden jogged into the water and swam to where Charlotte was.

"Jayden what are you doing, get out of the water. Get out of the water now," Carol yelled.

"Carol, relax." Jayden treaded water as she faced the beach. "Charlotte really is super friendly. There's no reason to be afraid of her." Jayden turned and closed the distance between her and Charlotte. She flipped over on her back and let Charlotte swim up on her belly. "I owe you extra veggies today," she said to Charlotte in a low voice, "That was classic. Scaring her was much better than biting her toes like we originally discussed." Charlotte blinked, and Jayden interpreted that as a knowing wink.

"I'll go grab her some veggies if anyone wants to help feed her," Taylor called over her shoulder as she sprinted to the cottage. She returned and handed pieces of pre-cut vegetables to all the outstretched hands and told them to follow her into the water. Everyone but Carol did just that.

As Jayden listened to their chattered excitement, she couldn't help but smile. It wasn't quite the morning she'd envisioned having after an amazing night of sex, but it was perfect in its own way. No one was hurt, and everyone looked happy. As she watched Taylor instruct them on how to hold the veggies so Charlotte could safely take them from their hands, her heart melted. She was in love with the most amazing person she had ever known, and life didn't get much better than that.

Twenty minutes later, when all the veggies were eaten, Charlotte made one more swim around the group, ducked her head under the surf, and vanished.

As everyone made their way back to the beach, one bride turned to Taylor. "So far, this has been the best wedding I could have ever imagined."

Taylor smiled back. "I'm glad you think so."

The group made their way up the beach and to the house, leaving Taylor and Jayden alone on the shore.

"Well, well, well, I bet they give the B and B a glowing, five-star review." Jayden placed her arm around Taylor's waist and leaned into her. She was proud of her. After months of hard work, she had really turned the place around.

"I sure hope so. We could use some more bookings."

"They'll come. Trust in the power of the lesbian grapevine."

"True." Taylor chuckled as they made their way back to the cottage. "I, um…" Taylor turned to face her. "I didn't realize how much you and Charlotte have bonded."

"She's my workout companion every morning, and I like to think she's watching out for me while I'm in the water. In exchange, I feed her breakfast."

"Speaking of, you hungry?"

"Starving." Jayden turned and kissed her. They still needed to have the *does this make us girlfriends* post-sex talk. But for now, Jayden was enjoying basking in the glow of a night of incredible love making.

❖

The rest of the day went by in a blink. After the wedding party cleaned up and left for their daily adventure, Jayden and Taylor decided to head over to Paia, the hippie-ish little town on the other side of the island. An art gallery there was showcasing a local lesbian photographer selling a series of underwater women-on-women prints. Jayden had seen an announcement of the exhibit on a flyer she'd picked up while standing in line at the drugstore, and she'd liked what she saw. Two topless women underwater in a sexual pose, surrounded by colorful fish, with a crystal-blue ocean backdrop had caught her attention. So much so that she couldn't stop talking about it. Taylor was the one who suggested they go check it out, and afterward, they could grab a nice lunch, get a massage, and linger in Paia for the afternoon. Jayden thought it sounded like the perfect day.

As soon as they stepped into the modest-sized gallery, Jayden fell in love. The store was colorful in an earthy, crunchy kind of way and only carried local art. Jewelry and trinkets lined tables, and paintings of all sizes and mediums covered the walls. They meandered through the store until she found what she was looking for. Seven prints of various topless women representing all shapes and colors came alive in the depths of the water. Jayden loved them all, but the one she'd seen on the flyer captivated her the most. As she stepped closer to examine the photo, Taylor came up behind her and wrapped her arms around her waist. She leaned back into Taylor's body and felt a shiver go up her spine. God, this woman gave her the feels.

"Is that the one you like?" Taylor said softly in her ear.

"Yes, I think it would look great on the one wall in the main room of the house." Jayden stared at the two women underwater in an embrace similar to the one they were in. Their hair and bodies were free from the pull of gravity, and right behind them was a sea turtle. "But it's a bit pricy."

"What on this island isn't? Besides, Frank is paying for it, and I so enjoying spending his money on stuff like this."

"You sure?"

"Yes, and besides, we're helping support a local artist." Taylor flagged the saleswoman over, whipped out her credit card, and asked if she could keep the print at the shop while they walked around town. The woman assured her it would be no problem.

They headed across the street to a quaint patio restaurant that advertised Mediterranean Italian cuisine. They spent two hours drinking wine, eating, and getting to know each other that much more. After dessert, they headed over to a spa and booked ninety-minute Swedish massages, which put them both in a blissful coma. From there, they ventured to a coffee house and relaxed even more, lounging around a patio with lattes in hand.

Jayden took a sip of coffee and let out a contented breath. She thought the day was as perfect as a day could be. And it was exactly what she needed to take her mind off the two questions that had been smashing around in her head since last night. Were she and Taylor a couple? And what about the divorce?

"What a wonderful day," Jayden announced as they entered the cottage carrying the over-sized framed photo. "I'll put the print in the bedroom until we can hang it in the main house. Meanwhile, pick out a good who-dun-it."

"Me?"

"Yes, and it has to have another super sexy woman in it."

"No pressure there at all." Taylor chuckled as she picked up the remote.

"Did you find one?" Jayden asked as she stepped out of the bedroom and contently wrapped her arms around Taylor.

"Sexy female cop with a cute partner, and according to the description, it's an exciting and unpredictable murder mystery with a twist."

"Sounds perfect." Jayden leaned her chin on Taylor's shoulder. Their bodies fused together in what Jayden thought was the perfect fit.

Taylor turned and gave her a soft kiss. Jayden replied by placing her hand behind Taylor's neck and bringing her in for a deeper one.

"If we keep this up, we'll never start the movie," Jayden moaned as her body began responding to the anticipation of being touched.

"Murder mystery first, then sex." Taylor pecked Jayden playfully on the lips.

Jayden let out a shaky breath as she calmed herself. As much as she was sexually aroused, she was equally exhausted from the day. Maybe a movie and cuddles would recharge her batteries for what she hoped would be another amazing night of love making. "I'll pop the popcorn, you relax."

"I don't think I could be any more relaxed."

She poured the kernels in the air popper, then leaned against the wall. "Thank you again for a wonderful day. I can't really remember the last time I enjoyed every single minute of an entire day."

"Well, the day isn't over yet." Taylor winked.

"Promises, promises." She unplugged the machine, grabbed the bowl and salt shaker, and walked into the main room. "How much salt?"

"A lot."

Jayden shook the canister until Taylor said it was enough, then settled next to her.

"Ready?" Taylor pointed the remote at the TV.

"Fire away." Jayden reached in the bowl and grabbed a handful of popcorn. She cleared her mind as much as possible. She wanted to be in the moment with Taylor and just enjoy the blissful feeling of relaxing next to the woman she loved. Nothing in either of their lives needed tending to right now. It was just the two of them, a bowl of popcorn, and a movie. Simple yet perfect.

❖

Halfway through the movie and well into their second bowl of popcorn, a back-alley mugging came on the screen. Taylor's heart started to race, and sweat beaded on her forehead. She tried to separate the scene that was unfolding in front of her eyes from her own nightmare, but the triggers were already pulled. She leaned forward, her breathing heavy as she bent her head toward her knees.

"Taylor, what's wrong? Baby, what's happening?"

Taylor couldn't talk; she just kept breathing deep, trying to take in more oxygen. She needed to breathe her way through this, but it was too late. She flashed back to that night. Fear gripped her as she relived the man jumping out in front of her. The stench of alcohol on his breath as he grabbed her shirt and demanded her purse. And feeling so terribly helpless.

"Taylor?" Jayden placed her hand gently on Taylor's back.

Taylor leapt off the couch and tumbled to the floor when her legs hit the corner of the coffee table.

"Taylor," Jayden said in a smooth voice. "Talk to me. What's going on?"

As the mugger on the TV loudly demanded the woman give him her money, Taylor placed her hands over her ears and squeezed. Jayden glanced at the screen, then back to her. "Oh my God," she said as she fumbled for the remote and quickly clicked off the TV. "It's okay, it's okay. Listen to my voice, Taylor, it's Jayden, you're okay."

Taylor took a moment to glance around the room. *You're in the cottage, you're safe, no one's here that will hurt you.* She repeated the statement over and over in her head until her heart rate returned to normal, and her breathing calmed. She jumped up. "I, um…"

Jayden held up her hand. "Whenever you want to share, I'll be here for you."

Taylor nodded. "Thanks, I, um, I think I need to go for walk."

"I'll go put on my—"

"Alone, I need to go for a walk, alone."

"Oh, well yeah, okay." Jayden slowly sat. "I see," she whispered as she looked down.

"Sorry," Taylor said. "I seemed to have ruined movie night."

"You didn't ruin anything. I figured out who did it a while ago. Take your phone with you, just in case." Jayden grabbed Taylor's phone off the coffee table and held it out. "Please."

Taylor nodded as she took it. "Thanks." She turned, headed for the door, and a second later, she was outside.

Her body was tense as she paced tight circles in the sand. *What just happened?* She hadn't had a crippling panic attack like that in a while. Tears began clouding her vision. When was she ever going to be free of that night? Her mind still held every moment so clearly. Every smell, taste, and sound. And every time a trigger knocked on that memory door, she relived the horror over and over again. It was something she would have to live with the rest of her life because every moment of that night was seared in her brain. Her pacing intensified as the adrenaline continued to surge through her body until she couldn't take it any longer.

She sprinted full speed down the beach. Running from her attacker, running from fear, and running from a past that would always be a trigger away from taking her back to that night.

Her toes dug into the soft sand as the fine grains separated under her weight, causing maximum resistance. She called upon every muscle in her body to propel her forward and out from the grip the sand had on her. The grip that *he* had on her. Her body responded to her call as she pumped herself forward, faster and faster. She wasn't thinking anymore; she was just responding. Her body became the machine she'd built it to be, and it gave back the one thing that Taylor needed most…strength. The one thing that had failed her that night so many years ago.

Strength was her drug. She needed it, was addicted to it, feared the day when old age would take all she had built. She knew of nothing else that could beat back the demon of her nightmares.

Taylor had no sense of time as she ran. The only thing she was aware of was her heavy breathing and the pounding of the waves that sounded like war drums in her head. She blocked out everything else. She was in her zone, and the only thing that got her out of her zone was burning exhaustion, which she was now feeling in her legs. Her muscles were on fire and starting to lock up a bit as she began to stumble in the sand. Her body might be a machine, but it had its limits. She dropped to her knees and rocked back on her butt. Her heart rate was so elevated, she could barely catch her breath. But at least the demon was gone. Chased away again...for now. She had won another round in its haunting.

She took a minute to collect herself, then slowly peeled her body from the sand. She looked around, and a slight panic gripped her. She had no clue where she was or how far she had run. She took several deep breaths and let the cool ocean breeze wash over her. She concentrated on the waves crashing on shore to help calm her. Her bearings were totally off. Fortunately, she had only run in one direction, so it would be easy to retrace her steps. She turned around and set a slow pace as she jogged back to the cottage, back to Jayden, and back to a truth she was not ready to face. What was she going to tell Jayden when she returned?

She reminded herself she didn't owe her or anyone else an explanation. Still, there was a part of her that wanted to bury herself in Jayden's arms. To share the nightmares of her life. Maybe doing so would lessen its power over her. But opening up to people left her vulnerable. And sadly, it was the first place they stabbed their criticizing dagger when pointing out her flaws.

She flashed back to when she'd told her grandfather of the mugging. He'd ridiculed her, planted seeds in her head that had cast doubt on her own actions and behavior. As though she had somehow caused it. He'd taken what happened to her and turned it against her. If her own flesh and blood could throw it in her face, who could she trust?

She cursed the nightmares, cursed the demon, and cursed all the relationships she'd lost because of its ripple effect. But more than that, she cursed herself for not being able to trust anyone enough to feel vulnerable again.

Taylor took a few moments and paced around the outside of the cottage. She needed to apologize to Jayden for her behavior, but at the same time, she really didn't want to talk about it. She scrubbed her fingers through her hair. She was tired of this pattern. Tired of getting close to someone and then pulling away.

She had hoped moving to the island would help bring new and happier beginnings. In a lot of ways, it had. Jayden's face flashed in her mind as she slowly opened the front door. The question was, what was she going to do about it?

Jayden was sitting on the couch with her phone clutched tightly in her hand. She jumped up and approached with open arms. But Taylor took a step back. She might want new beginnings, but right now, she still had old feelings causing her to emotionally retreat.

"I, um, maybe for right now, I could have a little space," she said in a low apologetic voice. She knew she was throwing a cold shoulder in Jayden's direction, and she felt awful about it. Jayden didn't deserve that. She deserved the truth, but Taylor was still on edge, and fear and flight were just under the surface of her skin.

"Oh, I, uh, of course, anything you need." Jayden stared through bloodshot, puffy eyes. Eyes that were melting her heart.

"Thanks, Jayden. I um, earlier, it was—"

Jayden shook her head. "Talk to me when you're ready."

Taylor put her head down and nodded. "Thanks." She stood frozen. She wanted to fall into Jayden's arms and cry. But instead, she turned inward. To a place she had created for self-protection when triggers were pulled, and life was too hard to deal with. It was a lonely place, but it was familiar. And right now, it was calling to her.

❖

Jayden felt like she was being kicked in the stomach. Something inside her said whatever she thought might have started between them had just ended. "Why don't you go take a long shower and get some of that sand off?" Jayden choked out as a lump lodged in her throat.

"I can just wipe down in the bathroom."

"Taylor, don't be silly. You're completely covered in a layer of sand and sweat. Now, please, go take a shower."

Taylor kept her head low and she whispered a thank you, then shuffled into the bathroom. As soon as Jayden heard the water run, she fell onto the couch and cried. Taylor was shutting her out, moving away from her touch, and closing off. She knew the signs. She'd experienced them from past lovers right before they'd broken up with her. That moment of realization when the woman she'd once made love to now felt repulsed by her touch. She brought her hand to her face and wiped the tears away. It was obvious Taylor was struggling with a past trauma, and it ripped her apart that Taylor wasn't talking about it because the one thing Jayden understood was nightmares. And the physical and emotional scars they left behind. If only Taylor would talk to her. But Jayden knew it wasn't that easy. Wounds healed in their own way and time. And it was clear to her that Taylor's were still raw. She wrapped her arms around herself and let out a gut-wrenching sob. How could their relationship survive if Taylor wouldn't let her in?

It won't.

❖

Taylor stripped her clothes off and stepped into the warm spray of water. She took a moment to stand there and let the water wash away the sweat and sand. Five minutes later, she reached for the bar of soap and slowly started rubbing it across her body. The scent of lavender filled the shower and brought a slight smile to her face. Jayden always smelled of lavender.

How could she have done this to Jayden when she knew better? She was a broken person, and Jayden deserved someone better. Someone who didn't come with nightmares locked inside, constantly banging against a cage, trying to get out. They should have never made love. Their relationship would never work, and tonight was a reminder. Taylor leaned against the tile wall of the shower, placed her hands over her face, and sobbed. She wanted love to return to her life. She wanted to feel as she once had in the arms of her mother. Protected and safe. Loved and cherished. *Where did that go?* But more important, was she so broken that she would never get it back?

She finally emerged from the shower when the water turned too cold to tolerate. As she stepped out and reached for the towel, she noticed a pair of her boxer shorts and a fresh T-shirt neatly folded on the sink for her. Taylor's heart saddened. *She's a better person than me.*

Taylor dressed and walked back to the main room. Jayden was sitting on the couch scrolling through her phone. "Feeling better?"

"Yes, thank you," she said more to the floor then to Jayden. Her stomach churned, and she began feeling nauseated. It was time to say the words she didn't want to say but felt as though she should. For Jayden's sake, she convinced herself, she needed to let her go. "I think tonight it would be better if I slept on the couch." Tears welled in her eyes as she made a promise to herself. No matter what it took, or how long, she would find a way to heal. She just wasn't convinced she could focus on that and a relationship at the same time.

❖

And there it was, the answer that punched the breath out of Jayden's lungs. She took a moment to absorb the words, turning each one over in her head several times.

They were no longer lovers.

"Oh," Jayden finally breathed out. "Of course." She stood and scooted the coffee table away from the couch.

"That's okay. I can get that," Taylor said.

Tears filled Jayden's eyes, and she didn't want to look up from her task and let Taylor see her pain. "Okay, then," she choked out. "I guess I'll just go to bed."

Jayden scooted past Taylor as she headed to the bedroom. She flopped in her bed, curled in a fetus position, and let the tears drip on her pillow.

It didn't take a rocket scientist to figure out that Taylor had a reaction to the scene in the TV show. Something bad had happened to her, and everything inside Jayden wanted to slide under the covers of the pullout bed and wrap Taylor in her arms. To protect her from whatever or whoever had hurt her. She replayed Taylor's first reaction when Sam had tried to hug her, and Taylor had always kept a safe distance from him. Her stomach began to cramp as she thought about Taylor going through her pain alone. She wished Taylor would let her in enough to help. Even if Jayden didn't know the exact words to say, she could still be there for her. Let her know in all the other ways how much she cared. She brushed another tear off her cheek. But then again, maybe Taylor didn't think she was worthy enough to share something she obviously guarded on a deeper level than the intimacy they had already shared.

Her mind went to the countdown clock. They would be divorcing in a few short months, and the thought of that caused a second wave of tears to fall. Jayden wiped her head on the pillow. When she'd agreed to this scheme, she'd thought the year in Maui would help heal her leg. She didn't realize how the time here would also help heal so much more. Although her heart was breaking right now, at least it was beating again.

CHAPTER ELEVEN

Jayden's head was pounding as she rolled over and tried to open her eyes. She had a crying hangover, and she felt like shit. As her brain slowly woke, it replayed the scenes from last night and reminded her why she felt like a train had run over her. "Taylor," she said in a low voice as she smelled coffee brewing. She rounded the door, and her heart sank. The couch was made, and a white bakery bag sat by the coffee pot. Her stomach was still too upset to eat, so she chose caffeine over sugar for her morning buzz.

She cupped the mug, stepped out on her front porch, and flopped in the patio chair. She took a moment to glance at the house. Taylor's truck was gone. She took a sip of coffee, closed her eyes, and willed her head to stop throbbing.

"Hey."

Jayden smiled. *Taylor?* She opened her eyes and frowned. "Oh, hey, Carol, what are you doing here? I thought you guys were doing the road to Hana today?"

"Yeah, everyone's on the porch ready to go. We're just waiting for our ride to get here."

"Well, have a wonderful day." *Now, shoo fly.* Jayden dismissed her with a wave. She heard the sound of crunching gravel as a van slowly pulled up in front of the house.

"Carol, the ride's here," a voice from the group called.

"Okay, be right there." Carol shouted, then turned back to Jayden. "So, um, I was thinking, maybe before I leave, we could go out for dinner?"

Jayden raised her left hand. "I'm married, remember?"

"Yeah, no, I mean, of course Taylor can come too. I just thought—"

"Carol!"

"Coming," Carol yelled, then turned to Jayden. "I just thought it would be nice to catch up and maybe, you know, work on a friendship."

Jayden glanced at Carol in disbelief. The woman who'd dumped her for not being good enough for her now wanted a friendship? She shook her head. "I don't know, Carol, it's not like we ended on the best of terms."

"I know, I know, just think about it, okay?" Carol called as she jogged back to her group. Jayden watched the women pile into the van, and as the vehicle pulled out of the driveway, she saw them chatting up a storm.

She sat back in her chair as she thought about Carol's request. It had taken her a while to find herself after Carol had systematically torn her to shreds and left the pieces scattered around for her to pick up and glue back together. And now she wanted to do dinner?

"Ha." Jayden snorted in distrust. Another power play by a woman who could teach a master class on manipulation. She took another sip as she weighed Carol's offer. On the one hand, if she said yes, she was signaling to Carol that she was willing to set aside the anger and forgive. On the other hand, if she said no, she was being a bitch for not even trying.

Maybe Carol had changed? "Nah," Jayden whispered to herself. If not for this unexpected encounter, she doubted Carol would be thinking about her at all. *Some people really are meant to be in your rearview mirror.*

Besides, right now, she needed to focus on Taylor.

She picked up her phone and sent Taylor a text, then glanced around the yard. Her eyes teared up as she thought about how much she was going to miss this place. It really did feel like home.

After being glued to her phone all morning, Jayden's worry over Taylor morphed into irritation. *It's a simple text, Taylor. It takes all of, what, a few seconds to reply?* She grabbed her phone and began typing another text, this one with much more edge in it, then thought twice about it. She frowned as she watched each letter vanish when she held the delete key. *Fuck this.* She changed into her board shorts and long-sleeve surfing shirt and stuffed the snorkel bag full of veggies. She was late for her morning swim, and she wondered if Charlotte would even be around.

She stood at the water's edge, scanning for any sign of Charlotte. She sighed when she didn't see any. She waded into the surf, and a few strokes later, she was in her usual spot, treading water. Her body was sluggish and slow. This was definitely one of those mornings that she wanted to do nothing but feel sorry for herself. She knew from Taylor's lack of a response that her role in Taylor's life had changed. Yeah, this was going to be a long day.

Twenty minutes later, she decided to call it quits. She wasn't in the mood, and it showed in her workout. Well, the word *workout* was a bit of a stretch. Floating in the water didn't really constitute exercise. She turned her back to the beach, closed her eyes, and slowly kicked her way to shore when she bumped into something. Fear gripped her as she jerked her body around.

Jayden smiled. "Thought maybe I wouldn't see you today. Sorry I'm late with your breakfast." She pulled out a head of romaine lettuce and handed it over. "So," Jayden began. "Wanna hear the latest? Taylor is missing. Well, not missing in the sense that I don't know where she is...well, I mean, technically, I don't know where she is, but I mean, she's missing in the, *she left without telling me where she was going,* sense of the word. Not that she owes me that."

Jayden rambled as Charlotte finished her lettuce. "But you would think that after making love, certain unspoken expectations automatically applied, right?" Charlotte cocked her head. "I have a really bad feeling about this, and I hope I'm wrong because I don't think my heart could handle it."

Jayden grabbed a few slices of red pepper and handed them over. "That's the last of it for this morning." She held up her empty hands. "See, no more." Charlotte bobbed in the surf for a moment, then slowly swam two circles around her and swam away. Jayden stayed in the water as she watched the huge sea turtle disappear and wondered where she went, if she had a daily routine or other turtle friends. She would never know the answers to any of these questions, and that was okay. Whatever Charlotte did and whoever she did it with, Jayden was just happy to be part of her life.

She waited until the van returned and deposited the happy wedding group back to the house before she ventured out to eat dinner at the patio table. Despite her somber mood, it was a beautiful clear night, and the stars were so bright, she felt as though she could reach up and touch them.

The sound of the waves slapping the shore was soothing, and the veggie burrito she threw together was actually quite tasty. She activated her screen. Still no text from Taylor. Funny how silence could say so much.

As she took another bite, she caught a dark figure in the corner of her eye. "Taylor?"

"Nope, just me." Carol stepped from the darkness and into the soft light of the porch. "I noticed Taylor's truck was gone and then saw you sitting out here alone and thought maybe you could use some company." She pulled over the other chair and sat. "You know, you could have let me know you were flying solo for dinner tonight and taken me up on my offer."

"I was actually enjoying having an evening alone." Jayden plopped her food on her plate as the word *alone* bottomed out her stomach. She'd lost her appetite. She felt miserable and pathetic sitting there waiting and wishing that Taylor would come home. "How was Hana?" She took a gulp of wine, hoping it would drown her sorrows. Between Taylor missing and Carol hovering, her mood had gone from miserable to irritable.

"Beautiful and amazing."

Jayden nodded. She had not been there but had heard enough about it to have a good understanding of the small quaint town at the end of a long windy road known for its one-way bridges, hairpin turns, beautiful waterfalls, and unique beaches.

"I felt a bit motion sick at times, but the payoff was worth it."

Jayden took another gulp of wine as they sat in awkward silence until Carol finally spoke. "So you're happy, huh?"

And there it was, the fishing pole was out and the lure cast. "Very." She tilted her mug back and chugged the last of the wine. Her heart was aching, and all she wanted was to fall into Taylor's arms and be told everything was going to be okay.

Carol folded her arms across her chest as she raised her right eyebrow.

"What?" Jayden asked because, dammit, she knew that look, and she knew Carol had this freaky weird radar when she sensed bullshit.

"Really?"

Jayden squared off with Carol and folded her arms across her chest. "What do you want, Carol, and why aren't you enjoying the evening with your friends?"

"I just spent all day in a van with them. I wanted to get some air and take a walk."

"So take a walk," she snapped. *And please leave me alone.*

"Ouch, when did you get so bitchy?"

Jayden sighed as she pinched the bridge of her nose. Deep down, she knew the anger she was taking out on Carol had more to do with herself. She was reliving the reality of being dumped by her ex-love while fearing her current lover was about to do the same. The irony of the situation did not go unnoticed. She softened her tone. "Carol, what are you hoping to—"

Jayden turned at the sound of a car come down the driveway. She watched Taylor stumble out of an unfamiliar vehicle and walk a bit unsteadily toward her. She could smell alcohol on her as she paused before heading into the cottage.

"I see Carol is keeping you company tonight." Taylor huffed but didn't wait for a reply as she opened the door and walked in.

Jayden scooped up her plate and mug and turned to Carol. "We're done here." She followed Taylor into the cottage.

Taylor was banging around the kitchen, opening and closing cabinets as Jayden sat. "What are you looking for?"

"Wine."

"On the counter by the toaster."

"Ah, there you are." Taylor grabbed the bottle and held it up. "Would you like some?"

"Already beat you to it, and whose car was that?" she said in an accusatory tone as jealousy raged through her.

"Uber. My truck's still at the restaurant." Taylor muscled the cork off and filled a mug. "I thought that was the safer call." She flopped on the opposite end of the couch. "What?" she asked as she took a gulp of wine.

"I never heard from you, so I was starting to get pretty worried."

"I'm…" Taylor lowered her gaze. "Sorry."

Sorry? Sorry? All day I have been worried sick over where you were, and all you have to say is sorry? Oh no, we're not doing this. We're going to have a real conversation about what is going on between us. "I think we need to talk."

Taylor nodded. "You start."

"Okay, well, um, first of all, I know we had an agreement that there would be no strings attached, and the marriage would be nothing more than a business deal."

"Correct."

"I need to know if that's still how you feel." She held her breath as she stared at Taylor. If she said yes, Jayden was convinced she would crumble to her knees.

Taylor placed her mug on the coffee table. She scrubbed her fingers through her hair. "I'm broken, Jayden, as in unfixable. I've ruined every chance of ever having a relationship, because I'm emotionally unavailable."

"Taylor—"

"No," Taylor cut her off. "Listen to me. I have a nightmare that will always haunt me, and as long as that's the case, it's not fair for me to get involved with anyone. You're amazing, Jayden, you're beautiful, funny as hell, and probably the sweetest person I know. You deserve to be with someone better than me."

"Please don't tell me who I should or shouldn't be with." *And please tell me this is not happening.*

Taylor sighed. "Jayden, there will always be a part of me that's running away because there will always be something in my life that will trigger a reaction. And that reaction will cause me to withdraw, sometimes for hours, sometimes for days, sometimes even longer."

"You're not the only one with nightmares, Taylor. Don't you think I've relived my accident over and over? I have woken in the middle of the night screaming because I think I'm still in the car. Spinning out of control while metal crunches around my leg. Every time I take a step, I'm reminded of that day. It's something that I'll have to live with the rest of my life, but it doesn't mean I have to let it control my life."

"It's not the same. I was…"

"Was what?" she snapped, then let out a long sigh as she pinched the bridge of her nose. She didn't want to fight with Taylor or even plead her case. This wasn't about her struggles; this was about Taylor, and right now, she needed to listen. "Talk to me, sweetie. We can work through it," she encouraged in a soothing voice.

Taylor abruptly stood. "I...I..."

Jayden watched her eyes well with tears. She wanted to pull Taylor into a tight hug, shower her in kisses, and tell her everything was going to be okay. That what they had started was worth fighting for.

"I...can't," Taylor said in a soft voice as she lowered her head.

"Taylor, how can you heal if you don't talk about it?" She knew from her own experience that the nightmares would probably never totally go away. But it wasn't about that. It was about Taylor trusting her enough to let her in and not push her away.

"I have my ways of dealing with it."

"Taylor—"

"What do you want from me, Jayden?"

Jayden wanted to say that she wanted everything and nothing at all. That she wanted to wrap her arms around Taylor and never let her go. That she wanted to make insane love to her every night and wake up to scones and coffee every morning. "I want..." She searched Taylor's eyes for a crack in her armor. She needed to know that she was willing to fight for this relationship. To fight for her. "I want..." She stumbled on the words again as she continued to search for any sign that Taylor wanted to be with her. But there wasn't any. Her face remained expressionless.

Jayden bowed her head in defeat. She was not about to beg someone to be with her. And as much as she loved Taylor, she knew that she could not save Taylor from herself. "I want what's best for you, but I don't want to be with someone who doesn't want to be with me." She was not going to have a repeat of Carol. She got up and hurried into the bedroom, shut the door, and let the tears flow.

❖

"Jayden," Taylor called. "Jayden." She crumbled to the couch, threw her head back and sank deep into the cushion. She closed her eyes and let a tear escape. She'd spent the day hiking, hoping the time alone would help her work through the hurdles she seemed to keep throwing in her own path. It was another pattern she always fell into the day after a meltdown: isolate, overanalyze, stuff the emotions back into a box, deny, repeat.

She was a jumble of emotions, and she was getting tired of her inability to work through them. She had spent years training her body to overcome the pain of physical exhaustion, to tear down a muscle and rebuild it stronger. If her physical strength led, her emotional state would follow. But that wasn't true. She spent so much time nurturing her physical health, she'd let her emotional health deteriorate. And now her life was a train wreck, and she had no idea how to get it back on track. Or even if she could.

Was it finally time to reach out and let someone in? To allow herself help in the one part of her life that she had made no gains? And acknowledge that doing so did not mean she was a failure? She rocked forward, grabbed the mug of wine, then thought twice and put it back down. She was numb enough. In fact, if she was honest with herself, part of her had been numb for the past several years.

She glanced over her shoulder at the bedroom door. The urge to snuggle with Jayden and tell her everything was tempting. Doing so wouldn't make her a weak or vulnerable person, but instead made her…what? *Trusting* was the word that came to her mind. She stood and stepped toward the door but retreated and headed for the kitchen. She needed to clear her head. She downed a glass of water and leaned against the counter. It was time to get her shit together. Since she couldn't change the past, she needed to figure out a way to change her future. What good was strength when she still cowered to the nightmares?

Maybe Jayden was right. Maybe she did understand more than what Taylor gave her credit for. Her heart softened as she thought of Jayden's pain. Could she heal with Jayden? But to do so, she would have to open herself up enough to let her scared inner child out. And it had been a long time since that part of her had seen the light of day.

CHAPTER TWELVE

Jayden checked into a hotel for the next three days even though the wedding party was departing in two. She needed time away from Taylor and especially time away from Carol. She made Taylor promise that she would feed Charlotte every morning, a promise Taylor said she would gladly keep. For the next seventy-two hours, Jayden busied herself as much as possible by playing tourist. She went to the aquarium, signed up for zip-lining, took a dolphin excursion, and attended the hotel's nightly luau, complete with fire performers and hula dancers.

She crammed as much as she could into those three days. She wanted to be so distracted and exhausted that she couldn't feel anything. The morning she returned to the cottage, the wedding party was long gone, and Taylor had moved her stuff back into the main house.

Jayden threw her overnight bag on the floor by the couch and flopped down. She was asleep within minutes. A knock jolted her awake. She stumbled to the door, hoping it was Taylor but instead found Sam standing there.

"Aloha, can I come in? I bring delicious gifts." He held up a bag of scones and two coffee cups.

"Hmm, food bribery." She stood her ground as she blocked the door. "Well played, Sam, but before I let you pass, you have to riddle me this…what's today's flavor, and what's in the cups?"

"Coconut glazed orange." He lightly shook the bag. "And medium roast almond milk cappuccinos." He raised the cups.

She stepped aside. "You've said the magic passwords. You may now enter."

He walked past her and over to the couch. He set the bag and cup on the coffee table, then turned and opened his arms. She hesitated at first, then fell into his big bear hug and snuggled in. "It's nice to see you again." She sniffled as her emotions came out.

"You too," he said in a soft voice as he held her tight.

She broke the embrace, flopped on the couch and motioned for him to do the same. She pulled out a scone and napkin and handed them to him. "Here you go."

"Thanks." He bit into the pastry. "It's nice that the wedding was such a success, huh?"

"Yeah, they seemed to love it here." She was sure this was the first of many to come, and that made her both happy for Taylor and sad that she would not be a part of them.

"What's not to love?"

"Did Taylor tell you one of the bridesmaids just happened to be my ex?"

"No." He leaned back.

"Yeah, and she kept approaching me saying she wanted to"—Jayden made a one-handed air quote—"catch up for old times' sake."

"And?"

"And nothing. Some bridges are burned beyond repair." A slight twinge of guilt hit her for not saying good-bye to Carol, but a quick flashback to the day Carol coldheartedly moved out put that guilt to rest.

"Probably a wise move." He shoved the last of the scone in his mouth. "You know, it's none of my business what happened between you and Taylor, but if you ever want to talk, I've been told I'm a good listener."

"She told you?"

"Taylor?" He snorted. "I think we both know she keeps me at arm's length."

"Then how did you know something had happened between us?"

"I overheard her on the phone talking to someone."

Annie. At least she's talking to Annie.

"But prior to that, I kinda figured it out when I asked about you, and a sad look came over her face when she told me you decided to get a hotel room and play tourist for a few days."

Jayden perked up a bit when she heard Taylor was sad. Maybe the days apart would bring them closer together? If Taylor had missed her as much as she'd missed Taylor, maybe there was still hope? But then again, if Taylor really wanted her back, why didn't she call or text? "Thank you for the offer to talk, but there's really nothing to talk about. I think it's safe to say the divorce is on track once Taylor gets the deed."

Sam frowned. "How much longer?"

"We were married February second. Once we cross our one-year anniversary, the lawyer will overnight the deed. Then we file for divorce, and I go back to my other life." As much as it stung to say those words, she had better start getting used to it. Like it or not, the second half of her roundtrip ticket was coming up.

"Well, I hope you know that I will really miss you."

She reached for his hand and cradled it in hers. "And I will miss you. This place is magical to me, and leaving it will be very hard."

"No chance that you could stay on?"

She shook her head. "It would be up to Taylor, but no, that wasn't what we agreed to. She made that very clear from the start."

"Well, then." He nodded. "We will focus on the time you have left. Gotta get your ukulele skills up before you return to the upper forty-eight."

Periodically, Sam would get out his ukulele, sit on the porch, and sing. His voice was soft and whispery, and it calmed her when she listened. She had always wished she could carry a tune, but she was on the complete opposite end of that spectrum.

When she was younger, her mom had enrolled her in piano lessons. Learning to read the notes was easy enough, that was just memorization. But translating those dots and symbols into music was something completely different. It was a talent a person either had or didn't. And she definitely didn't have it.

Jayden smiled. "Maybe instead, I can just listen to you play." No sense continuing the lessons. It wasn't the instrument; it was her. Why waste time on something that was never going to change?

He stood and rounded the coffee table. "I should probably get back to work. Taylor wants me to build a koi pond." He opened his arms, and she once again fell into his embrace.

"A koi pond? Where?"

"Off the side of the house by the keahi tree. She wants a pond that has boulders for a waterfall and all that stuff. I called a buddy of mine who said he can build it."

"Sounds beautiful."

"Yeah, I guess."

"You don't sound thrilled."

"I don't know anything about ponds, and I'm sure the maintenance of it will fall on me. I'll feel bad if any of the fish die."

"I'm sure you'll do just fine." She walked him to the front door. "Thanks for stopping by and bringing me breakfast. I think I'm going to head out and swim with Charlotte in a bit. I'll tell her you said hi."

"She's a sweet old soul." He walked past her and out the door.

"That she is," she said as she caught a glimpse of Taylor bounding up the porch steps. She was returning from her morning run and Jayden had to fight back the urge to grab her coffee and stroll to the house. "No," she whispered as she returned to the cottage. She wasn't going to chase her. Taylor either wanted her or she didn't. Another reminder not to waste time on something, or someone, who was probably never going to change.

❖

Taylor was in a cranky mood. As soon as she entered the house, she glanced at the print that she and Jayden bought in Paia and could feel it mocking her. Reminding her of what she could have had, had she been capable. *After the divorce, I'll have the print wrapped up and shipped to Jayden.* She didn't need a reminder of that day hanging over her head.

She went into her bedroom, plopped on her mattress, and threw her arm over her eyes. She wanted Jayden to leave the island. She *needed* her to leave the island. Every moment she was still here was throwing Taylor off-balance. She shouldn't have slept with her. As amazing as it had been, it was a stupid mistake. And it was tearing Taylor apart. She had never felt this out of sorts after sleeping with someone. It was new, and it scared her. Falling back into old patterns had always worked in the past, but this time it wasn't coming so easy. She needed to feel as though she was back in control of her life. Not the chaotic emotional mess she had become. *What's so different about this time?*

Her phone rang, and she figured it was probably Sam with another question about the koi pond. Why in the hell had she ever decided she wanted to build one? Oh, yes. She smirked. Distraction. She reached in her pocket and fingered her phone out. It was Annie. "Hey," she croaked.

"Uh-oh, someone doesn't sound good."

"Sorry, Annie, I'm just not having a good morning."

"Feel like talking?"

"Not really."

"Okay, I'll talk."

Taylor sighed. She already knew what Annie was going to say. "Fine, you talk."

"You know I love you to death, and there isn't a thing in this world that I wouldn't do for you."

"I'm sensing a *but*."

Annie took a moment before she spoke. "But prior to what happened the other evening when you were watching TV with Jayden, I've never heard you so happy. So full of life."

Taylor closed her eyes as tears dripped onto her pillow. "You of all people know what a wreck I am." Her voice cracked. "I just need more time to figure it all out." She repeated the same broken excuse that she had been telling herself and Annie for years.

"Taylor—"

"I know what you're going to say, and you're right. But it doesn't mean I'm ready for it."

"I just want to see love in your life. You deserve it, and I think with Jayden, you could have it. She's a good person, Taylor."

Taylor felt the sting of those words because truthfully, she felt the same way. That was why shutting Jayden out hurt so much. But Taylor also knew what letting her in would do, and she didn't want to inflict that on Jayden. Taylor came with baggage. A hell of a lot of baggage. And so far, none of her past lovers were able to handle that load, and with each breakup, it forced Taylor deeper and deeper into an emotional cave. Happily-ever-afters were for people who had a sense of happiness to begin with. That wasn't her. She was a guarded person, someone who was always looking over her shoulder. *Tense* was the word her lovers used. Someone who just couldn't lighten up enough to enjoy life's simplest pleasures.

"Just do me a favor," Annie said. "For the remainder of the marriage, don't push her away."

"What makes you think I'm doing that?"

Annie laughed. "Oh please, you're probably avoiding Jayden like the plague and secretly wishing she was already gone so you don't have to be reminded of what a nice person she is. Am I right?"

"Maybe." Taylor sighed. Annie knew her well.

"Sweetie, how many times have you promised me you'd get therapy?"

Taylor remained quiet. She knew Annie was going to bring this up again, and she knew she was out of excuses. Between her grandfather and the mugging, she was long overdue. She just always thought she could fix it on her own, grunt her way through it and end up stronger. But clearly, that had not happened.

"I know, I know."

"I think now might be a good time to actually do it. Promise me?"

"I promise." And for the first time, she meant it. No matter how much she wished she could do it on her own, she finally conceded that she needed help.

"You know I'm only ragging on you because I love you."

"I know. I love you too."

"Mom says hi, and she told me to tell you she's thinking she'll feel well enough to fly soon."

"Annie, that's awesome."

"Yeah. I'll give you some dates soon so we can make plans. Gotta go for now. Remember your promise. Love you. Bye."

"Bye." As Taylor hung up, she did actually feel better. She typed therapist in her phone, and several in the area popped up. She took a few moments to open their websites and read their profiles. One in particular stood out. She hovered her finger over the appointment icon, but as anxiety gripped her, she closed down the site and promised herself she would make an appointment later.

Why is it so hard to take the first step? She remembered several of her clients at the gym talking about how hard it was for them to finally sign up for a membership. When she'd asked them why, some said they didn't think they needed to until it was painfully obvious. As she headed for the kitchen to make a fresh pot of coffee, those words echoed in her head. She knew she had reached the painfully obvious stage, and it was finally time to do something about it.

Chapter Thirteen

Jayden was glued to her phone. According to the National Hurricane Center, the powerful Category 3 storm was packing maximum sustained winds of 129 mph and heading dangerously close to the Big Island. A hurricane watch was issued for Maui and other smaller islands. Damaging winds and heavy rainfall were expected to affect portions of the Hawaiian Islands for days, and flash flooding and landslides were predicted.

Two days later, the all-day rain, strong swells, and dangerous surf arrived. Jayden worried about Charlotte as she listened to the intensity of the waves crashing on the shore and hoped she was safe.

By that evening, ferocious winds lashed across Maui, toppling trees and knocking out power to the other side of the island. The wind was so fierce, she thought the cottage couldn't possibly withstand it. She longed for the safety of a basement as she nervously sat on the couch, scrolling through the local news feeds on her phone.

When she first heard the pounding, she thought the wind had knocked a tree branch against her door. But when she heard the muffled sound of Taylor calling her name, she soon realized something was wrong. She hurried to the front door and opened it as the wind pulled the knob out of her hands and slammed the door against the wall.

"Taylor, what is it, what happened?" She reached out and pulled her into the cottage.

Taylor was hunched over and drenched from the rain. "Something happened to Sam," she yelled over the deafening sound of the howling wind. "He sent me a text that said help. I called him back several times, but he's not picking up. I'm heading over to his place to see if he's okay."

"I'm going with you." She ran into the bedroom, threw on a pair of jeans, and returned to Taylor. *Please let him be okay.* She exhaled a shaky breath and stumbled a bit in her step as the walls of the cottage felt like they were closing in on her. Adrenaline and fear combined as her heart rate accelerated.

"Jayden, I don't—"

"I said I'm going with you," she repeated as she pushed past Taylor. If Sam needed help, she was going to do everything in her power to give it to him. "Let's go," she shouted. She bent forward as she struggled to advance against the surging wind. As soon as she jumped in the truck, she retrieved her phone, hit Sam's contact information, and let the app provide directions.

"Did his text say anything else?"

"Just help." Taylor threw the truck in drive and headed to the other side of the island. She leaned forward over the steering wheel. The wipers moved across the glass like a hyper metronome.

As they ventured inland, the wind and the rain intensified. Sam's side of the island was definitely getting the brunt of the impact of the storm. "Damn," Jayden whispered as she glanced at the pooled water on the side of the road that was only inches away from flooding the highway.

Gusts of wind slammed against the side of the truck, rocking it as the rain continued to explode on the windshield. The soft calm voice coming from Jayden's app told them to take a right at the next light. As soon as Taylor did, Jayden felt the backend of the truck fishtail a bit before catching.

Jayden's muscles tightened, and her stomach flinched from fear. She instinctively reached out and placed her hand on

Taylor's thigh and squeezed, hoping it would steady her nerves. She knew venturing out under these conditions was foolish and dangerous. But if Sam was in trouble, what choice did they have? "I'm scared."

"We'll be okay," Taylor reassured her.

What should have been a twenty-minute drive took them over an hour as Taylor had to make several U-turns and find alternative routes due to downed trees.

"Holy shit," Jayden whispered as a cold chill came over her, and a sour taste made its way up her throat. Raging water was pummeling the far side of Sam's tiny house as the ground under the foundation was rapidly torn away.

Taylor threw the truck in park and jumped out. "Get in the driver's seat," she yelled over the wind, "and be ready to move the truck if you need to. I'm going into the house. Start honking if things out here get worse."

Jayden jumped out and rounded the truck as Taylor ran past her. "Be careful," she yelled as she helplessly stood and watched the darkness and rain engulf Taylor. She fought the urge to run to her, hold her in a protective embrace, and feel Taylor's lips on hers one more time. She wanted to tell her she was scared that something bad might happen to her. And if it did, she would be forever lost without her. Her stomach tensed as she watched her walk into a situation she might not walk out of, and fear and anxiety gripped her. She jumped into the driver's seat and drummed her fingers nervously on the steering wheel. "Come on Taylor, get them out of there." *And please come back to me.*

❖

"Sam," Taylor yelled as she approached the house. Adrenaline pumped through her body. She was spooked and on edge. She had no idea was she was about to walk into, and her mind raced with worst-case scenarios. She took a deep breath to steady her nerves and calm her mind.

"In here!"

She could barely hear his plea as she hopped on the porch and opened the front door. A rush of water poured out of the house, pounding into her legs and almost knocking her feet out from under her. She gripped the door frame to steady herself, and as soon as the surging water eased, she waded through ankle deep water as she made her way into the house.

"In here," Sam repeated, a desperate cry for help.

Taylor rounded a corner and saw him pinned under a solid-looking entertainment unit. A frail woman—probably his grandmother—was leaning over the furniture in a half-soaked pink-flowered housedress. Her hands were on the corner as she tried to move it.

"Sam!" Taylor rushed over to him and bent down as a tightness gripped her chest. She quickly assessed the situation as a manic energy pulsed through her. "Talk to me." Her words broke as she placed her hands on the unit to get a feel for the weight.

"The house shifted, and this thing came crashing down on me. I'm okay, but I can't get out from under it." He struggled.

Taylor positioned her body in a squat stance, reached under the water until she felt the edge of the unit, and tightened her grip. "Okay, lift with me. Ready…one, two—" The house's foundation shook as if an earthquake was splitting the land under it. A large crack appeared in the wall, and plaster from the ceiling showered down on them. Taylor lost her balance and splashed backward in the water. "Oh shit," she mumbled in a daze as she focused on the widening split in the wall. She sat frozen. Her heart pounded in her ears. A chill tickled its way down her, and she shivered. They needed to get out of the house. Now.

A deep-throated sound snapped her back and caused her to turn. Sam's face was flushed deep red, and his arms began to shake as he tried to lift the massive piece of furniture. *Sam!*

She jumped to her feet as she quickly recovered and repositioned herself in another squat. "Okay, ready…lift." She grunted. "Push!"

But the furniture would not budge.

"Shit." She released it. Her muscles were burning as she stood and shook out her legs and arms.

"Taylor," Sam said in a desperate voice as another large piece of drywall dropped from the wall and splashed in the water next to them.

"I know. I'll get you out." She placed her body in another full squat position, plunged her hands under the water, and gripped a different part of the unit. "Again, Sam, ready…lift!" Taylor closed her eyes and gritted her teeth as she screamed in pain. But the unit was too heavy for her. She just didn't have the strength to move it. "No," she called to herself and refused to give up. She was not going to let something defeat her again, never again. She flashed back to the night of the mugging, the night her body had failed her. "No," she repeated as she began to shake. *Never again, never…*

She let out a breath and focused on her legs. She blocked out the burning and tearing sensation of her muscles and thought of nothing but the simple act of standing. *Just straighten your legs and stand.* The trembling and shaking set in as her muscles began to tighten and cramp. The pain that shot through her was so intense, her eyes began to water. *Just stand up.* Taylor took another deep breath and held it as she heaved one last time. And then she felt it. It was slight and almost imperceptible, but it was movement none the less. "Now, Sam, now!"

He released his grip on the furniture, and scooted out. "Clear," he yelled as he tried to stand but tumbled to the floor in a splash. His grandma waded through the water and tried to help him up.

Taylor dropped the unit and stood frozen, her muscles so spent she couldn't move. Her chest heaved as she gasped for breath. A sharp stabbing pain sliced through her thighs as the room began to spin, and her head pounded so much, it felt like it was going to explode. She needed to sit or lean against something and take the pressure off her legs, but as soon as she tried to take a step toward the wall, she heard the sound of honking.

"Jayden," she whispered. *Shit, something was happening outside, and whatever it was, it wasn't good.* Heightened adrenaline surged through her body. "We have to," she panted, "we have to go." Taylor took a step and stumbled into the water.

Sam reached out for her. "Can you walk?"

"Yeah, I'm a bit unsteady, but I can manage." She grabbed for Sam's arm, and he helped heave her up. She had to concentrate on moving her legs. They were locking up on her, and she was beginning to lose sensation in them. The honking continued as an uneasy feeling washed over her. "We gotta go…now." Taylor looked in Sam's eye's, and he nodded.

"Grandma, we have to go." He wrapped his arms around her as he limped out the door. Taylor was a few feet behind them, willing her body to move one foot in front of the other. She was desperate to get out of the house and get to Jayden. She needed to know she was okay.

"My tin." Sam's grandmother twisted in his arms. "I have to have my tin."

Sam made a motion toward her. "No, we have to go." He held her in place as she beat at his arm.

"No…my tin!"

"Your what?" Taylor asked as they reached the door.

"Grandma's tin, it's on the kitchen table. It's got all her memories in it." He turned and started heading back into the house.

"No. I got it, Sam, you guys get to the truck." She reacted without thinking. Through gritted teeth, she splashed into the kitchen and grabbed a small silver tin that sat in the middle of the table.

"Taylor, you need to get out here now," Sam yelled, as she forced her legs through the resistant pull of the water and out the door. The rain was coming down so hard, each drop felt like hail exploding on her skin.

Jayden jumped out of the truck, ran to the passenger side, and opened the back door. She helped Sam place his grandmother on the seat as the loud crash of a tree falling made them all look up. A large mango tree had lost its last grip on the earth and was now a part of a wall of debris that was heading right toward them. Terror gripped Taylor and in a moment of disbelief, she stood frozen. Was she really seeing what she thought she was seeing?

"Taylor," Jayden yelled over the wind and rain.

The sound of Jayden's voice snapped her back. "I see it, get in." She hobbled to the truck and jumped into the driver seat. Jayden hopped in the passenger side and Sam into the back. Taylor tossed the tin to Sam, threw the truck into drive, and floored the accelerator. The truck slid out from under them for a moment before it caught and propelled them forward. The tree slammed against the back-passenger side of the truck, causing them all to lurch sideways.

"Hold on," she yelled as she white-knuckled the steering wheel and pushed the accelerator harder into the floorboard. The tree shoved them closer and closer to the side of the mountain.

"Taylor." Jayden's voice was shaky.

"Come on, baby, come on." She urged the truck to fight its way out of the tree's grip. She pressed harder on the accelerator, but it was already flat against the floorboard. In a few seconds, the tree would have them pinned against the rocky wall.

"Taylor." Jayden repeated.

"I know." She was shaking from so much adrenaline rushing through her, and her leg began to bounce as it held the accelerator down. "Come on," she urged as she caught a glimpse of Jayden in the corner of her eye. If anything happened to her, Taylor would never forgive herself. "Come on," she yelled. The truck's wheels stopped spinning as they caught traction on a broken section of the pavement. The truck lurched forward, and the tree punched and scraped down the side of the truck before reluctantly releasing its hold. She glanced in the rearview mirror and watched the mango tree rapidly float down the street.

She reached over and placed a protective hand over Jayden's. "You okay?"

Jayden nodded.

"Sam?" She glanced again in the rearview mirror.

"We're fine, just get us out of here," he said.

"That's the goal." She exhaled as she leaned forward and drove as fast as she could down the mountainside. She became hyper alert as she dodged several more trees and earthly debris littering the roads. They weren't out of danger yet, and the responsibility for getting them back to the B and B safely weighed heavy on her. *You can do this.*

Sam called, "Go left, go right," as he directed her to the main highway.

By the time they pulled into the driveway of the B and B, the rain and wind were steady but not life-threatening. As soon as Taylor threw the truck in park, she released a long shaky breath and hunched over the steering wheel. She had never felt so exhausted. So totally spent. And a part of her wanted to just sit alone in the truck for a while. She needed to release the last bit of adrenaline still surging through her and a gut-wrenching cry was already building within.

Jayden placed a hand on her back and rubbed. "You okay?"

Taylor nodded but kept her head down. Tears began welling up in her eyes, and a lump stuck in her throat.

"Shit. Sam, let me help." She snapped her head up when she heard Sam helping his grandmother out of the truck. She wiped a hand over her face, leapt out, and stumbled over to them.

"It's okay. I've got her." He reached his arm around his grandmother's shoulder, and the two of them slowly shuffled to the house.

"Here." Jayden slid her arm around Taylor's back. "Looks like you could use some help too."

Taylor's first reaction was to jerk away. To remain in the truck and deal with her emotions on her own. Like she always did. But the warmth of Jayden's body leaning against hers melted her legs, and she easily fell into her arms.

"I have spare clothes that you can both change into," Taylor announced as she and Jayden made their way into the kitchen to join Sam and his grandmother.

"Don't think they'll fit me, but they'll fit Grandma. Just throw mine in the dryer while I take a shower, and that'll be fine." He leaned over and kissed the top of his grandmother's head. "Grandma, this is Taylor and Jayden." He nodded toward them. "And this is my grandma, Leilani."

"It's nice to meet you, Leilani." Taylor extended her hand. Leilani gently brought it to her face and rubbed it on her cheek. The intimacy of the gesture felt surprisingly calming to her, and she let her hand linger on Leilani's face.

"Okay if I jump in the shower now?" Sam asked.

"Um, yeah. Sure." Taylor mumbled as she stared at Leilani. There was something about her face that sent recognition chills throughout her body, but she couldn't quite place it.

"I'll put some hot tea on and make us something to eat," Jayden announced.

Sam hugged her. "Thank you, Jayden." He broke the hug, turned to Taylor, and took a step into her personal space. She stared at Sam, and the realization of almost losing him punched her in the gut. This beautiful person, who'd made their transition to the island so smooth and peaceful. Who introduced them to Charlotte and played the ukulele softly on the porch. And graced them with the best scones they had ever eaten. The thought of losing him was more than she could bear. She lowered her head and leaned into his warm embrace.

"You saved us," he whispered in a low emotional voice. "I will forever be grateful."

Taylor nodded as she choked back tears of her own. "Leave your clothes outside the bathroom," she said as she broke the hug. "I'll throw them in the dryer."

An hour later, they were all sitting around the kitchen table in dry clothes, sipping on hot tea, and eating the sandwich squares Jayden threw together. Leilani was looking at Taylor so intently, it was starting to make her feel a little uncomfortable. A few times, she brushed at her face to see if there was something on her cheeks or nose that no one was telling her about.

As Taylor leaned over Leilani to grab her mug and refill it, Leilani cupped Taylor's face and held it in a gentle and caring embrace. It was another intimate gesture, and she wondered again why she was the focus of Leilani's attention. She searched Leilani's eyes. *What is it about me that fascinates you so?* What was the woman of few words trying so desperately to say?

Taylor smiled as she placed her own hands over Leilani's. "I'm glad we were there to help you both. This place is yours for as long as you need to be here." She looked up at Sam. "Why don't you two sleep in the master tonight? I'll sleep in one of the upstairs bedrooms. You too, Jayden. I'd feel more at ease if we all were in the same place tonight."

Sam and Jayden started to protest, but Taylor held up her hand and shut them both down. "The master is on the first floor, Sam. I don't think either you or Leilani should tackle stairs right now. And, Jayden, I think the house is a bit sturdier than the cottage. I'd worry less about you if you were here."

Jayden smiled. "I actually would feel safer in the big house, closer to everyone. So thank you."

"All right, then, it's settled. We'll figure out the rest of the details tomorrow. For now, though, let's just stay together, get as much sleep as possible, and regroup in the morning, okay?" Until the storm passed, she still felt the need to protect them, especially Jayden. She had seen the fear in her eyes and heard it in her voice. If anything had happened to her, Taylor would never be able to get that out of her head, and she would always feel responsible for causing it.

Sam leaned over and helped Leilani off the chair. He grabbed her tin, and the two of them shuffled to the master bedroom. The sight of a big bear of a man wrapping his arm around a frail and petite woman was precious.

"Use whatever you need in there," Taylor called as she watched them disappear into the bedroom. Exhaustion finally caught up with her, and she slumped into a chair as uncontrollable tears dripped on the table.

Jayden pulled up a chair next to her and brought Taylor into a warm embrace as she leaned into her. "You okay?"

"The furniture was so heavy, I almost couldn't lift it. What if I…what if I hadn't been able to free Sam?"

"But you did, and now everyone is safe…and home." Jayden whispered.

Taylor sobbed as she dug her face into Jayden's arm. Tonight had been a close call. Her body had almost failed her, and in turn, she could have lost someone important. As she tightened her embrace with Jayden, she cried even harder. She cried for the loss of her mom, the loss of a life she felt robbed of, and the loss of the start of what could have been the best relationship in her life.

❖

Jayden reached out a hand. "Come on, let's get you to bed." As she led Taylor up the steps, she reflected on the night: the surge of nightmares that came flooding back the moment the tree hit her side of the truck, the gut-wrenching fear that another tragic accident was going to take even more from her. With that vision in her mind, she gently squeezed Taylor's hand. She could have lost her tonight, and she needed to be reassured by Taylor's touch that they were safe, and all was okay. That this time, they had been lucky. "Which room do you want?" she asked as they stood in front of the first bedroom off the stairwell.

"This one's fine." Taylor nodded.

"Then I'll take that one." She pointed to the one across the hall. As Jayden turned, Taylor asked in a soft voice. "Would you…would you mind if we held each other tonight?"

Jayden glanced at Taylor and saw what seemed like a look of vulnerability. "I think that would be nice."

They walked to the bed, pulled back the covers, and flopped in. As the wind began to die down and the sound of the surf once again became their background music, Jayden stroked Taylor's head. She thought about the first day they'd met at the gym and all the conversations they'd had while she exercised on machine after machine. She thought about the wedding and the seashell Taylor had given her, and then her mind lingered on the night they'd made love.

As exhausted as she was, her body responded to the visions she conjured in her head, and every sensation she'd felt that night came rushing back. She tightened her thighs but was careful not to do anything as she sensed Taylor's breathing change to a slow, deep rhythm. She wanted Taylor to sleep tonight, and as she let out a long slow breath to steady her desires, she closed her eyes and concentrated on feeling the warmth of the person she loved lying next to her. She tried to stay awake as long as possible so she could treasure this moment, but within minutes, she too, was sound asleep.

CHAPTER FOURTEEN

Taylor jerked awake and took in her surroundings. Images of the storm, Sam, Leilani, and Jayden smashed into her brain. She turned her head and saw Jayden peacefully sleeping next to her. She had been so tired by the time they'd walked up the stairs, her memory of them going to bed was a distant blur.

She sat up on her elbows, glanced at the window, and squinted. A patch of sunshine was shining in. She slipped out of bed as quietly as possible, but Jayden stirred. "What time is it?" she mumbled.

"Too early. Go back to sleep."

Jayden cracked an eye open. "Where are you going?"

"To pee and see if Sam's up. Go back to sleep."

Jayden closed her eyes and mumbled something incoherent as Taylor headed for the hall bathroom. She wanted to turn, kiss her on the cheek, and let her know she was grateful Jayden had been by her side last night. That it meant a lot to her. That she meant a lot to her. But instead, she decided to let her sleep.

It took her a minute to get down the stairs. Her body was sore, and her muscles ached, a reminder of the hell they had just been through. As she headed to the kitchen, she noticed the master bedroom door was wide open. As she went to close it, something caught her eye.

Leilani was sound asleep on her back, softly snoring and clutching an old black and white picture of a man, woman, and baby. A jolt of recognition shot through Taylor as she focused on the man in the photo. What was Leilani doing with a photo of her grandfather?

Sam strolled out of the bathroom. "Uh oh." He hurried her out of the room and into the kitchen.

"Why does your grandmother have a picture of Frank?" And who was the woman and baby? She had always been told her grandmother died giving birth to her mom, so none of this was adding up. A sick feeling came over her. Did her grandfather have another family she knew nothing about?

"I can't tell you." He pulled out a kitchen chair and sat.

"You can't tell me why a picture of my grandfather is clutched in your grandmother's hands? Really?" Taylor sat next to him. She felt a little betrayed by his flippant answer. She viewed Sam as a friend and thought he felt the same about her. So why the secrecy?

"Taylor, it's not mine to tell."

"So you do know?"

He let out a sigh. "Grandma was going to tell you. She just first needed to know you were safe."

"Safe? From what? What the hell is going on, Sam?"

He looked down. "Your grandfather kept a secret from you."

"Apparently, he had several." She huffed as she gestured to the house.

"This one tops them all."

"Morning." Jayden yawned as she came in. "Wait." She paused. "What did I interrupt? I'm sensing something is going on here?"

"Leilani has a picture of Frank with a woman and a baby, and Sam knows about it, but he won't tell me."

"It's not that I won't. It's that I promised I wouldn't."

Jayden pulled up a chair and joined them. "What's Leilani doing with a picture of Taylor's grandfather? Did they know each other?"

"I'm so sorry. I can't tell you."

Taylor shoved against the back of the chair in frustration and folded her arms across her chest. She glared at Sam as a flash of anger surfaced. She'd risked her life for him last night, and now he wouldn't give her the courtesy of answering a basic question about her own grandfather?

"Sam?" Jayden gently asked. "Why can't you tell?"

"Because I asked him not to." Everyone turned to the doorway where Leilani was leaning.

Sam helped her to a chair. "What can I get you, Grandma?"

"Coffee would be great. Then could you please go get my tin?"

Sam froze.

"It's okay." She shooed. "You were right, she has a right to know. I've allowed Frank's threat to silence me for too long, and that's something I'll always have to live with, but Taylor has a right to know." Leilani turned to face Taylor. "I'm so sorry."

Sam placed a mug in front of Leilani, retrieved the tin, and sat. No one said a word as they waited in silent anticipation while she slowly took a sip of coffee, then with shaky hands, opened the tin. It was full of black and white photos mixed with washed-out colored ones. She sifted through them carefully, pulled out a dozen, and placed them on the table. Frank was in all of them.

"This is your grandfather and me." She flicked an old tattered black and white photo over to Taylor.

Taylor looked at her grandfather sitting next to a beautiful, young, petite woman on a bench, arm in arm.

"We were lovers, Frank and I."

Taylor jerked her head up from the photo. Her mind raced with a thousand and one questions, but as she opened her mouth to ask, Leilani held up her hand.

"It was after the war. Your grandfather was stationed in Oahu, where my family lived. Both of my parents worked in a local pineapple field. It's very hard work, and I swore I never wanted to follow in their footsteps and do that kind of labor…

ever. A friend got me a clerical job at the naval base, which of course, made my parents furious." She looked up from sifting through the tin. "Hawaii was still a territory back then, and my parents thought the US military was exploiting the islands. They asked me over and over again to quit my job, but I refused."

She paused as she took another sip. "That's where I met your grandfather. He was handsome and charming, and it didn't take long before I was lying to my parents about what I was doing after work. I knew they would not like me hanging around with a military boy, so I never told them about Frank. But then I became pregnant, and I couldn't really hide the truth anymore."

She shook her head. "I knew it wouldn't go over well, and at one point, I thought about running away. But where would I go? So I told them, and although they were not supportive of my relationship with Frank, they honored and loved me enough to stand by me. But Frank and my parents did not get along. He started saying really horrible things about them and my people. It led to a lot of fighting between us." She sighed as she glanced at Taylor. "I eventually quit my job and gave birth to a sweet baby girl, and my heart was never fuller. She was perfect in every way. When she was six months old, Frank told me that he had orders to return to the States and asked me to go with him."

Tears filled her eyes as Sam reached a caring hand over to hold hers. "I told him I couldn't. I just couldn't do that to my family. Besides, I wanted my daughter to be raised on the island, exposed to the ways of her people. Frank said he wanted her raised in the States, far away from our culture." She wiped a tear from her cheek. "We broke up that night, and Frank said he wanted nothing to do with me or our daughter, but he was lying. The evening before he was to ship out, he contacted me and begged to see me. He said he wanted to say good-bye, and he insisted I bring our daughter. We met at a small diner. Halfway through the meal, I got up to use the restroom. When I returned, both Frank and my sweet baby girl were gone."

Leilani plucked another photo out of the tin and handed it to Taylor. It was the photo Taylor had seen clutched in her hand earlier. She pointed to the baby. "That was my sweet baby girl, my little Puanani…your mother."

Those words were like a punch to Taylor's stomach. My mother? Impossible. She shook her head in disbelief as she glanced at Leilani. "That can't be my mother. Frank told us that my grandma died in child birth."

"He lied." A deep sadness washed over Leilani's face. "When I came back to the booth, I was frantic. I stood staring at the empty table and started screaming. I ran out of the diner and drove to the military base. But they wouldn't let me in. They told me I was hysterical, and they threatened me. I tried to track Frank down. I wrote letter after letter to the government, but all of them went unanswered. My parents had no money, so we couldn't afford to fly to the mainland or hire anyone to find him and my sweet baby girl. A year later, I received a letter from a lawyer who represented Frank. It said that if I continued to try to find him, he would stop me from ever seeing Puanani again. The letter also said he would be in touch at a later date, but that date never came. It was the last time I ever heard from Frank, and my hopes of ever seeing my daughter again vanished as the years went by."

The room felt like it was spinning as the taste of bile made its way up Taylor's throat. She felt nauseated, and she started to breath heavy. She always knew her grandfather was a heartless bastard, but this was more than she could process.

"Eventually, I married a local man, which made my family proud, and I had Sam's father. But there wasn't a day that went by that I didn't pray to the stars to watch over my little Puanani and keep her happy and safe."

Leilani wiped the back of her hand across her wet eyes. "The next time I heard from Frank was when I got a letter informing me that your mother had died of cancer. In the letter was this picture." Leilani slid another photo across the table.

Taylor picked up the picture, and her breath caught. It was a photo of her and her mom, taken two years before her mom had died. The two of them were at the state fair, ice cream cones in hand and huge smiles on their faces. Tears formed as she closed her eyes and was instantly transported to that moment in time. Her mom had just been told she had breast cancer, and in a rare act of kindness, Frank had taken them both to the fair. They'd ridden rides, played arcade games, and ate junk food until they'd felt sick to their stomachs. It was the best memory Taylor had of the three of them together. "I remember when this was taken."

Leilani gave a knowing nod. "It was the first picture I saw of my Puanani all grown up and the first time I knew that I had a granddaughter." She glanced at Taylor. "There was no return address on the envelope, so I had no idea where you where or how to get in touch with you. Sam was the one who eventually found Frank. He got online and started doing searches. He found out Frank had a place in Indiana and this house on Maui. All this time, he was so close, and I never knew it."

"He never brought me or my mom here or even told us about this place," Taylor said as she traced her mom's image in the photo. Her heart was breaking. To know that her mom and her grandmother were torn apart and kept from each other was beyond her comprehension.

"I'm sure he didn't want to risk anything that could expose his secret," Leilani said in a soft voice. "Anyway, Sam took it upon himself to confront Frank. Since he lived on this island and I was still on Oahu."

"I went to this house several times," Sam said. "But no one was ever here. Then one day, I knocked again, and he answered. I told him who I was and ripped into him. He just stood there, not saying anything. He finally turned and walked back inside, but he left the door open, so I followed him in. He said he figured someone would come knocking sooner or later. I told him Leilani still lived on Oahu and asked if he wanted to see her. He told me no, that he never wanted to see her. When I asked about his granddaughter, he just shrugged and told me that you two"—Sam nodded toward Taylor—"were estranged and that he didn't know where you were. We talked for over an hour that day, and when I was leaving, he turned and asked me what I did for a living. When I told him I was in between jobs, he offered me this one. He said he'd hire me, but Leilani could never set foot on the property. I told him where to stick it and then called Grandma. She told me to take his offer. That in doing so, maybe I could learn more about where you were in the hope that someday, we would find you. But Frank never talked about you, not once."

Not once. The words echoed in Taylor's head. So many emotions were surging through her, she thought she would explode. A combination of anger and hurt turned into a shot of adrenaline as she started to bounce her legs.

"Anyway," Sam continued, "last year, when Grandma's mobile home park was bought up by developers, I moved her in with me."

Taylor couldn't stand it any longer. She stood and paced the kitchen. "To my mother's dying day, she thought she'd indirectly contributed to your death." Taylor scrubbed her fingers through her hair. Her heart rate accelerated, and it felt as though she was suffocating. She needed to get out of the house and run until her legs could no longer carry her, to be alone with her thoughts and emotions. She needed to do what she always did: retreat until the pain was no longer gripping her, and she was back in control. "And Frank just sat back like he got off on it in some weird twisted way."

"Frank punished me for not choosing a life with him," Leilani answered. "He punished my parents for not accepting him, and he punished my sweet Puanani because she reminded him of it all."

Taylor stopped pacing, leaned against the countertop, and kicked her heel into the cabinet. "God, he was such an asshole!"

Leilani walked over to her. She cupped Taylor's cheek and gently stroked Taylor's face. "I spent my whole life praying that I would see my beautiful daughter again before I passed, and he took that from me. But now I know she lives in the soul of my beautiful granddaughter. You have your mother's eyes. Kind, sweet eyes that hold the wonder of the world in them. Welcome home, my Puanani, I've missed you so much." She leaned in and hugged Taylor.

Sam got off his chair and approached with open arms. "We're ohana."

Taylor nodded and waved him over. "Family."

Sam leaned into the group hug. "Yes. We're family."

"I saw it on a beach towel," Taylor mumbled into Sam's shirt as the realization of the word hit her. She had a cousin and a grandmother. A family she never knew until now. She was no longer alone.

Sam giggled. "Of course you did."

❖

As Jayden scrambled a large pan of eggs, she thought about Taylor. She had hoped after last night, the awkward space between them was lifted and that maybe Taylor would finally begin to open up and let her in. She'd seen a raw side of Taylor and knew from experience that crying it out was a big step in the direction of healing.

But now, with everything that had just been revealed, would Taylor shut her out even more? Jayden had seen firsthand how Taylor turned inward to process emotions instead of reaching out. She had hoped that in the end, she would be the one Taylor turned to when she finally chose to share herself. But as she scraped the eggs into plates and listened to Leilani and Taylor share stories about their past, a feeling of resignation came over her. Maybe for now, that wasn't her place in Taylor's life. Maybe that spot was reserved for someone else who needed healing on the same level Taylor did.

Jayden glanced at Leilani and placed a plate in front of her and smiled. By the time she placed the other plate in front of Taylor, she had come to the conclusion that she needed to step aside and let Taylor find a place in life and with her new family. If in the end, Taylor came back to her, Jayden would like to think she would still be around, somewhere…waiting.

She grabbed two more plates and motioned to Sam that they should head into the main room. She wanted to leave Leilani and Taylor alone and give them time and space to begin the process of healing and bonding.

Sam flopped on the couch, picked up the remote, and surfed between three local news channels. By the time they finished their breakfast, they learned the other side of the island had been hit the hardest, with massive power outages, flood damage, and property loss. So far, there was one reported fatality and dozens of injuries.

A news reporter stood by a barricaded street and rattled off a list of sections on the island that were inaccessible or too dangerous to enter. Sam's neighborhood was one of them.

"Hey, can I use your phone to call a neighbor and see if they know anything about my house? I can't find mine," Sam asked.

Jayden fished her phone out of her pocket and handed it to him. "Of course, use it as much as you want." She listened as he left message after message. He sounded more desperate with each call. She felt sorry for him, and a sinking feeling settled in. She was sure when the calls were finally returned, the answer to his questions would be heartbreaking.

She stood and arched her back. She needed a break from the news, and Sam looked like he needed a distraction. "I'm going to check the cottage for any damage and then walk the property. Wanna come?"

The sun was shining through patches of clouds, and the lingering smell of rain mixed with the cool air. As they strolled onto the deck, Sam whistled. "Damn." The yard was full of broken tree limbs and plant debris. Clean up would take time, but fortunately, nothing major seemed uprooted or damaged. As they hopped down the stairs, they got their first look at Taylor's truck. The entire passenger side was smashed in and scraped up.

Jayden carefully glided her fingers over the damaged metal as she remembered the terrifying moment the tree had slammed into them. The fear that had gripped her and didn't let go until they were back at the B and B. She said a silent thank you to all the forces of the universe that were at play last night that brought them safely home. She thought of Taylor asleep in her arms last night and added a p.s. *Double thank you for watching over the woman who holds my heart.* If anything had happened to her, Jayden wasn't sure she would ever get over it.

"It's going to take some serious body work to repair this." Sam said.

"Yeah," Jayden mumbled.

"If it's even possible," he added as he placed an arm on Jayden's shoulder. They remained silent as they turned and slowly made their way to the cottage. "I don't see any damage."

At first glance, Jayden thought the exterior of the place seemed to have weathered the storm just fine. "Me neither." She held her breath as they entered the cottage. Not one item, trinket, or picture was out of place. "Looks okay."

Sam glanced around. "The little place held up just fine."

"Yes. It did," she answered in a quiet voice as she slowly spun in a circle. The home she had become so fond of stood strong. She glanced at Sam. The thought that his home was either gone or damaged beyond repair saddened her. What would it be like to never be able to return to a place that held so many memories? She glanced at the print over the couch and thought of the night Taylor had stood in this exact spot and passionately kissed her. She would always cherish those memories of their time in her little cottage that soon enough, she too would never be returning to.

"What do you say we clean up the yard?" She needed to break away from her thoughts and welcomed a mundane task.

For the next hour, they dragged tree branches and limbs to the side of the house. As they raked the rest of the debris off the grass, they talked endlessly about Frank. And the more Jayden heard, the more disgusted she became. Sam filled her in with everything he knew. He told her about Leilani's fear that Frank, even in death, would have someone spying on Taylor. And if they saw that Leilani had come back into her life, they would somehow withhold money or make her life miserable in some other way.

Jayden wheeled a plastic trashcan over. "That's so sad."

"I know." Sam dumped a pile of leaves in the can. "She really didn't put anything past Frank, which is why she wanted to wait and make sure Taylor was safe from anything like that before she came forward and told the truth."

"Sam?"

"Hmm?"

"How could Frank afford a place like this?"

"His parents owned a small telephone company that was bought out by what eventually became AT&T. Between that and other investments, Frank's parents did all right. But they both died in an accident when he was a teenager, and I think it messed him up a bit." Sam stopped and wiped his face on his T-shirt before continuing. "Frank was an only child, so he got everything. He bought this place not long after he left the military."

"Wow," Jayden said, "all that money and he never shared it with his own family."

"Frank was definitely an ass and paranoid as hell. He was convinced that someone was going to take it all away from him. He didn't trust many people, and he basically hated everyone.

Except the military guys. He seemed to worship them." Sam shrugged. "But he could also turn on anyone in a heartbeat and be mean to the bones."

"Apparently, he—"

"Thought you guys might be thirsty." Taylor and Leilani emerged with glasses of iced tea on a tray.

As Jayden dropped her rake and headed for the porch, she watched Taylor's interaction with Leilani, and it warmed her heart. They already seemed comfortable and attentive with each other. "That looks wonderful." She hopped up the stairs, grabbed a glass, and moaned. "Oh, that really tastes good." She plopped on a lounge chair as her phone vibrated and displayed a number she didn't recognize. "This is Jayden." A man identified himself as Sam's neighbor, and from the little he said, she knew her hunch about Sam's house was right. "Hold on, please." She turned to Sam and held out the phone as a lump formed in her throat. "It's your neighbor."

Sam wiped his hands on his shirt and took the phone. "Aloha." Jayden watched his expression go from hopeful to despair in a matter of seconds. "Okay, thanks for letting me know…I'm glad you and Mary are safe…I'll talk to you soon. Mahalo." He handed the phone back to Jayden as he softly announced, "Five homes in the neighborhood were destroyed in the flood. Ours was one of them." He turned to Taylor. "We're homeless."

Leilani mumbled something in Hawaiian as she folded her arms around her chest.

"Oh, Sam, I'm so sorry." Jayden scooted her chair next to him and placed her hand over his. "You and Leilani can have the cottage if that's all right with Taylor."

Sam shook his head. "That's you're place, Jayden. And it only has one bedroom. But if you guys can watch over grandma until I find a place to rent, I would appreciate that. I'll go crash at a buddy's place until then."

Taylor scoffed. "You are not going to crash at a buddy's place." She leaned in and quietly said to Jayden, "You sure about the cottage?"

Jayden nodded. "I'll gather my stuff and move into a hotel."

"You're not going to a hotel. Pick a bedroom and settle in for the next couple of weeks," Taylor said. "As for you two"—she gestured to Sam and Leilani—"I'm giving you the cottage. Call your buddies, Sam, and have them give me a quote on building an additional bedroom and bath onto the cottage. I'll let you supervise it. The place is yours."

The next couple of weeks...Jayden repeated the words that caused her stomach muscles to tense and not in a good way. The divorce clock was still ticking loudly in her head. In just over two weeks, Taylor would have deed in hand, and Jayden would be gone. The place would be Taylor's, and Sam and Leilani would have the cottage. Their lives could begin here while hers ended.

Taylor stood and announced, "All right then, it's settled. Sam and Leilani will live in the cottage indefinitely, and I don't want to hear any pushback. Ohana, right?"

Leilani wiped a tear off her cheek as Sam stood. "I, um, don't know what to say. I'll pay rent, of course."

"You are not paying rent. This is on Frank. Payback for what he stole from each of us."

"Give me a few minutes to pack," Jayden said as she abruptly stood and headed to the cottage. Tears were starting to pool in her eyes, and she didn't want anyone to see her cry.

By the time she opened the cottage door, she was sobbing. She shuffled her way to the couch and did a face-plant into the cushions. She was glad to give up the cottage for Leilani and Sam. It was the right thing to do. They had been through so much. They had more right to this place than she did. But damn it, she loved the cute little house, the island, Charlotte, and Sam, and she was head over heels in love with Taylor.

"Get it together, Jayden." She sobbed as she pulled a tissue from the box on the coffee table. She knew that the first time she'd walked into this place, there would come a day when she had to walk out. With a heavy heart, she slowly stood. It was time to pack and say her good-byes to the little cottage that had given her so much joy.

She glanced again at the print over the couch, pulled out her phone, and snapped a photo. It wouldn't be worth the cost to ship it back to the mainland, so she would give it to Taylor. A reminder of the night they'd shared. Complete with love, free of nightmares, and full of so many possibilities.

❖

Sam turned to Taylor. "Are you seriously going to let her get away?"

"What?"

"Are you seriously going to go through with the divorce?"

Yes. No. Maybe. But the truth was, she didn't know. Her emotions were raw right now. She felt like everything was coming at her at once. There was so much to process that she was on sensory overload. She was still hurt and angry at Frank, she was excited about her new family, and she was sad that her mom wasn't here to be a part of it all.

Not to mention, she was in love with Jayden. Of course she was; how could she not be? Jayden was everything she wanted in a woman. The issue wasn't Jayden. It had never been her. It was Taylor. It had *always* been her. She was the broken one. The one who needed help but was too stubborn to ask. "It's what we agreed to." The words fell like a thud as soon as she said them. Yes, it was what they'd agreed to, but so much had changed since then and now. She only wished *she* had changed that much as well.

"For what it's worth, I think you're making a big mistake."

"There's more to it than you know, Sam," Taylor snapped. She didn't need another lecture on why she needed therapy. What she needed to do was go for a long run. The past twenty-four hours had been emotionally intense. She was wired and tired and was so far out of her comfort zone that she feared she would never get back to center.

"Well, unless either of you is a serial ax murderer, I can't see a single reason or excuse for not staying married. You two complete each other."

"Wow, so now that we're family, you think it's okay to play the role of the opinionated relative?"

"We've always been family, and you know I'm right," Sam shot back.

They were sparring, and she knew she wasn't going to win this round. Sam was right. Jayden did complete her. She just didn't think she could complete Jayden. *I just need more time to process everything.* She listened to the voice of the broken record again. She slouched and lowered her head. "Look, Sam, I've been down this road before, and the end result never changes."

"Well, maybe it's time to try a new road," Sam quietly replied.

She let him have the last word because she was starting to become tired of listening to her own excuses. Tired of repeating the familiar patterns and tired of herself. *Who am I anymore?* It wasn't the first time she'd asked it, but it was the first time she answered. *You're someone who self-sabotages love because you're too afraid to feel.*

CHAPTER FIFTEEN

Jayden pulled up to the curb at the Kahalui airport in a white Jeep. Taylor's F-150 was going to be in the shop for another three to four weeks, and fortunately, her insurance covered a rental. She threw the Jeep in park, jumped out, and gave Andy a big hug. "I've missed you so much."

"I've missed you more," Andy said as he gave her a squeeze.

They both anticipated that she would be a wreck after the divorce, so he had graciously flown out to stay the week and fly back with her.

Andy leaned back and gave her the once-over. "Oh my God, girl, what have you done to yourself? You look like a tropical goddess. I so want to be you right now."

Jayden playfully spun in a circle as she modeled her body. She had shed a few extra pounds in the past few days and not because she was trying to. She had lost most of her appetite leading up to this week as depression settled in.

She tossed Andy's luggage in the back seat and jumped in. Within minutes, they were on the road to the B and B. She inhaled a deep breath and exhaled a deep sadness. The next time she went to the airport would be to catch her own flight home. Where had the year gone?

"I'm not kidding. You really look great. I mean, the selfies you've sent me don't do you justice," he said as he powered down the window.

"Thanks, Andy. Being able to swim every day has really made all the difference. I'm going to have to find a gym with a pool when I get back." Besides, there was no way she could ever set foot in her old gym again without thinking of Taylor.

"Fitness 24 on Elm St. My coworker goes there. They have a lap pool and everything, but the monthly dues are a bit pricey."

"That's okay. It'll be worth it."

Andy leaned his head out the window. "God, the sun feels good."

"Yeah, but watch out, it can be intense at times."

"Please, I just left four inches of snow, seventeen degrees, and an ice storm on the way. Don't even talk to me about intense."

Jayden chuckled. She had not missed the brutal cold of Missouri winters at all. "It's going to be hard to leave." Impossible was the better word. But what choice did she have? She could never afford to live on the island. And there was a part of her that didn't want to unless she was with Taylor. Maybe it was good that Hawaii was so far away. A clean break was probably the only way she would ever get over her heartache.

Andy gently placed a hand on her thigh. "I know, sweetie, and I'm sorry."

"Nothing to be sorry for. That was the deal. I knew what I was getting into. I think I just underestimated how much I would fall in love with everything and everyone."

"Is Taylor still supposed to get the deed on Wednesday?"

"Yep. Everything's on schedule. Deed comes Wednesday, celebration that night, and divorce the next morning."

"You want me to go with you to the courthouse?"

She shook her head. "No, that's okay." But things were not okay. On that day, a piece of her heart and soul would be forever altered. Yet another life-changing event that would mark the time before the divorce and the time after.

The rest of the drive, she listened as Andy filled her in on the lives of their mutual friends. She'd missed watching Andy tell his stories in real time, with all the facial expressions, body language, and hand gestures that lacked in their phone calls and FaceTime chats. As she pulled down the gravel driveway and parked, she glanced over and watched him take in the sights. Goose bumps covered her skin as she remembered sitting in the passenger seat of a Jeep just like the one they were in and having the exact same expression wash over her face exactly one year ago.

"Holy shit." Andy's mouth dropped.

"I know, right?"

"Okay, I've only been here for a few seconds, and already I never want to leave."

She sat with him for a few more moments, taking it all in. A tear escaped and made its way down her cheek. This was going to be a rough week. During her time here, Jayden felt as though she'd found herself, and she feared how much of her would be forever lost when she left. Could she honestly go back home and pick up where she'd left off? Of course not. Something within her core had changed while on this island, and the only question that remained was how much of that change would stay with her.

"Come on," she finally said as she wiped away the tear. "Let's go introduce you to everyone." She hopped out and grabbed Andy's suitcase and coat. "Everyone should be in the kitchen making dinner." She led him across the lawn and to the porch.

"Oh, good, because the tummy is a rumbling."

The sliding glass door was open, so they walked right in. Taylor was the first to come out of the kitchen, wiping her hands on a dish towel and smiling. She approached Andy with open arms.

"Hey, Andy, nice to see you again."

He leaned in. "Thanks Taylor, you look fabulous," he said, then pulled out from the hug. "And this place is amazing."

"Gayest B and B on Maui," Taylor announced.

"It is now because the gayest of them all just arrived." Andy winked.

"Aloha, welcome to Maui. I'm Sam." Sam came up behind Taylor and extended his hand.

"Hi, Sam." Andy shook his hand. "I've heard a lot about you."

"And this"—Taylor walked over to Leilani, who was leaning against the door frame smiling—"this is my grandmother, Leilani."

Andy pulled her into a gentle embrace. "I've heard so many wonderful things about you. It's so nice to meet you."

When Andy broke the hug, Leilani reached up and cupped her hands around his face. "It's nice to meet you, Andy, beautiful friend of our sweet Jayden."

"I can already tell we're going to be best of friends."

Leilani, gave him a gentle pat on his cheek, smiled, and nodded. Jayden felt a stabbing pain to her heart as she watched the exchanges. This was Taylor's family, and as much as she wished she was a part of it, she wasn't. Even though she was sure they loved her as much as she loved them, she was beginning to feel like the odd one out again.

"Okay, big boy." She placed her hand on Andy's shoulder. "Let's show you to your room so you can get settled in."

"Dinner's in a half hour. You good with that?" Sam asked.

"I'll be dressed and ready," Andy said as Jayden led him up the stairs to his bedroom.

"My room's right across the hall." She pointed.

"You sure it's okay that I'm staying here?"

"Yeah, Taylor blocked all reservations for this week so we could all be together without any distractions from guests."

"That was nice of her."

Jayden nodded as she turned to walk away. "I'll give you your privacy. Come on down to the kitchen when you've freshened up."

"Will do."

"Andy's looking good," Taylor said as Jayden strolled into the kitchen.

"Yes, he does." She grabbed a stack of plates and started setting the table. "It's good to see him again."

"Behind you with hot lasagna." Sam reached around her as he placed the food on the table.

"That looks amazing," she complimented, even though she wasn't feeling too hungry.

"Well, Taylor made it. I just took it out of the oven."

"That smells delicious." Andy stepped into the kitchen. "What can I do?"

"Open the wine." Taylor handed him a bottle and corkscrew.

Within minutes the kitchen was full of chatter and laughter. Jayden leaned back in her chair and glanced around the table as she took a sip of wine. She was surrounded by the people she loved, and that thought brought her a sense of peacefulness. *This is what life is all about.* She smiled as she closed her eyes and wished, *if only time could stand still.*

❖

Late that night, Taylor stumbled into the kitchen for a glass of water and noticed a flickering light floating down the stairway. She quietly crept up the stairs and followed the glow into Andy's room. When she stepped into the doorway, warmth filled her heart. Jayden and Andy were propped up in bed, side by side, sound asleep with the TV still on. She felt a hint of jealousy shoot through her. Not because she had anything to worry about between Jayden and Andy, more because there was a part of her that wished she was the one Jayden was peacefully snuggling with.

She turned and walked back down the stairs as quietly as she'd come up. She could have that, she ridiculed herself. All she had to do was trust herself enough to let Jayden in. To know in her heart that she was not going to repeat her patterns, and in turn, hurt her. How was it that she could lift hundreds of pounds in weights yet couldn't seem to lift the hurdle that was right in front of her? The one she had been tripping over all these years? For all the strength she possessed in her muscles, she could really be weak at times.

The next morning, Taylor sat in the kitchen, eating a scone and going over the latest bid to expand the cottage when Jayden waltzed in. She seemed more relaxed and not as tense as she had been lately, and Taylor wondered if having Andy here was calming her. If so, she was thankful he could be there for her in ways Taylor couldn't.

"What's today's flavor?" Jayden asked.

"Macadamia nut with lemon glaze," Taylor said as she grabbed the bag from off the table and handed it to her.

"That sounds *divine*."

"Yes, I am, thank you very much," Andy announced as he strolled into the kitchen. He had on dark blue board shorts with light blue trim and a baby-blue, long-sleeve surfer's shirt. "And I am ready for my Maui debut."

"Oh, you have, um…" Taylor pointed to her face. "Your suntan lotion is…"

"What?"

She walked over to Andy and rubbed his face.

He jerked back a bit and playfully slapped at her hands. "What are you doing?"

"You didn't rub your sunscreen in well enough. You look like a ghost."

Andy gasped as he grabbed her hands and put them back on his face. "Fix it before I become a public embarrassment."

"Well, I don't think you'll ever be a public embarrassment, but there." She finished rubbing and stepped back. "Now you don't look as—"

"Dead?"

Taylor smiled as she sat back down. "Not what I was going to say, but I'll go with it. So…" She glanced at Jayden, then quickly turned away. She had noticed Jayden had lost more weight, and the sparkle in her eyes was dimmer. She knew that look because she had seen it on herself, and she understood the pain associated with it. And it saddened her that she was probably the cause of Jayden's pain. "Where're you two off to this morning?"

Jayden handed a scone to Andy. "First, we're going swimming with Charlotte, then this afternoon, I thought I'd take Andy for a full island tour. Maybe end up down on Front Street so he can see the banyan tree and do a little shopping."

"Sounds like a nice day," Taylor mumbled. And it did. She would love to hang out with them for the day. But she knew it would feel like torture, and she would be miserable. Because in the back of her mind, she would be feeling guilty that she was making another memory of something they couldn't have.

"You're more than welcome to—"

"No, thanks, you two haven't seen each other in a year. Enjoy catching up. I um…" She shuffled the papers in front of her. "I need to review the construction bid for the cottage." She looked down. She was both anxious and depressed that Jayden was leaving in a few days. She was logging two runs a day, and even with the extra miles, she was still having trouble sleeping at night. At this stage, she just wanted it over, and yet, she didn't.

Ugh, she was such a walking contradiction of emotion. She glanced again at Jayden's baby blues. Her heart melted, and her stomach did all the things stomachs did when they wanted to be with someone. Yet her head came swooping in and *whooshed* away the thoughts to replace them with doubt. Fucking head games. Well, one thing was for sure, she thought as she broke the stare, she loved Jayden too much to saddle her with the pile of broken pieces that had become her life.

Concentrate on fixing yourself first. It's the only way the pattern will be broken.

❖

"Okay." Jayden smiled and turned to Andy as the waves lapped around their feet. The water felt cool but nice. "Just follow my lead. Charlotte is super sweet and gentle, but be warned, she's a big old girl, so she can be a bit intimidating at first."

"I still can't believe you have a sea turtle as a pet and not something a little more conventional. I've seen plenty of feral chickens and cats running around. Didn't one of them do it for you?"

"Trust me, it's not quite the same." She walked farther into the ocean. "You'll see." She shook off a chill as the water splashed against her legs.

"Don't tell me you think this is cold." Andy walked right in without hesitating. "This feels like heaven compared to seventeen degrees." He dove under the wave, turned over, and backstroked out a bit.

"Showoff." She dove under the next incoming wave and swam over.

He treaded water. "You come out here every morning?"

"Every morning I can." She viewed her time in the ocean as not only her morning meditation but her therapy. The water soothed her soul, and talking things out with Charlotte helped soothe her mind. It was a routine that would be impossible to replace.

"I could get used to this."

"I know," she said in a soft voice as she sighed. "See why I fell in love with this place?" But it wasn't just this place. She was in love with who she had become here.

"Aw, sweetie, I'm sorry, I didn't mean to…what the fuck is that!" In one stroke, Andy was behind her, clinging to her back.

She tried to wiggle out of his grasp, but he had his fingers dug into her shoulders. "That's Charlotte," Jayden said, "and I can't get to the food if you insist on being a human backpack."

Charlotte approached and bobbed in the surf. "Hey, Charlotte. How's my baby girl doing this morning?"

"That's Charlotte?"

"Yeah, and I need to get her food, so you need to get off my back, Andy."

He let loose his grip but maintained a close proximity. "You didn't tell me she was sea monster status."

"I told you she was a big old girl." She held out a clump of lettuce, and Charlotte bit into it. She flashed back to the first day she was introduced to Charlotte and remembered how terrified she'd been. A good reminder that the outside didn't always match the inside. "Sometimes we aren't who we seem, huh, old girl?"

"Sweetheart, we have different definitions of what a big old girl looks like."

"What were you picturing?"

"A sweet and cute sea turtle of manageable size with a big butt."

"Turtles don't have butts." She put a piece of lettuce in Andy's hand. "You can feed her. She's very gentle."

Andy released the lettuce. "First of all, everything has a butt, and second, I do love the fact that my fingers are still attached to my hands, so I think I'll pass."

Charlotte swam over to the loose lettuce leaf and chomped on it. "You have to admit, she really is beautiful." She focused on the waxy, rubbery look of her head and the dark eyes that spoke to her. Beauty might be in the eye of the beholder, but no one was going to convince her that Charlotte was anything less than gorgeous.

"In a sea monster kind of way, I guess."

"I'm really going to worry about her when I'm gone."

"Will Taylor feed her?"

"Yeah, she and Sam both promised that she will continue to be spoiled beyond words."

"Then it sounds like you have nothing to worry about."

No, Jayden thought, she wasn't worried about Sam and Taylor feeding Charlotte. What she worried about was that they wouldn't talk to her. And most of all, she worried that Charlotte would wonder where Jayden was and feel a bit abandoned. She was convinced they shared a special bond, and she didn't want Charlotte to feel like she'd broke that by choice.

The next seventy-two hours were a whirlwind. Jayden took Andy to as many tourist spots as she could. She wanted him to get as much of the island experience as possible in his few short days. Plus, the distraction was welcome. The divorce clock was now ticking so loud inside her, it had become a throbbing headache. Playing tourist was the only thing that seemed to give a little reprieve from the constant reminder of what was to come.

On the fifth evening, everyone was sitting around the front porch, eating ono tacos and drinking wine. Tonight, they were celebrating deed day. It marked Jayden and Taylor's wedding anniversary, plus one day. The day she had dreaded. She was up all night tossing and turning different scenarios. What if she and Taylor had never crossed the line? Would Taylor have let her stay here in some capacity? But what would she do? And more than that, could she really be around Taylor and not act on her feelings? Suppress them? No. And why would she want to? What kind of pathetic life would that be? Begging and hoping that the woman you loved would finally see you?

Taylor had confessed that she was broken. Well, who wasn't? Why couldn't they just work it out together? Was it really that hard? She glanced over at Taylor and swallowed the lump forming in her throat. She felt like she had waited her whole life for a woman like Taylor to come along. Now that she'd found her, she didn't want to let go. But what choice did she have? None. She took another gulp of wine and welcomed the numbness that was beginning to set in.

"Time to move on," she whispered to herself. But how was she supposed to take that first step forward when her heart kept pulling her back?

"Open it." Sam gestured to the sealed mailer sitting in the middle of the table.

Taylor stood, placed the envelope to her chest, and took a breath. "Okay, here goes."

Sam beat his fingers on the table to sound like a drum roll. Taylor grabbed the pull tab and dramatically ripped open the package. Jayden held her breath as Taylor sifted through the paperwork. Maybe the deed wasn't in there? Maybe something else came up that said they needed to stay married for a while longer? But a heartbeat later, Taylor presented the deed for all to see, and Jayden's stomach bottomed out.

Sam stood as he raised his wineglass. "May the magic and the spirit of the island always be a part of this house and all those within."

Jayden raised her glass and took another big drink. Right now, the only thing she wanted to feel was nothing at all.

Andy plopped next to her on the lounge chair. "How you doing?" He nudged her gently on her shoulder.

Jayden forced a smile. "Fine. Numb." She took another gulp. "I'm happy for Taylor, really I am, I'm just—"

"Madly in love?"

"Yeah. I know this sounds cliched, but I really don't know how I'm going to find another woman like her."

"You won't. You'll just do what we all do when our hearts get broken. You'll get on with it because you know deep down, you'll never get over it."

"Yeah." She glanced down and started to twirl her ring. As long as she had the ring on her finger, she felt connected to Taylor. She slid it to the tip of her nail, willing herself to take it off but couldn't. She slid it back and sighed. She would wait until tomorrow to hand it, and her heart, back to Taylor.

❖

Taylor stared at the deed, and sadness filled her. She thought of her mom. Her beautiful mother who had struggled her whole life and never had the opportunity to call a place her own. She thought about the late nights they cuddled on the couch as she jabbered about everything and nothing at all and the sacrifices she'd made for Taylor and the unconditional love Taylor could always count on. And how her mom would tell her over and over again to stay true to her heart. "A heart is meant for love," her mom would say. "Never let hate take hold." And with those words echoing in her mind, Taylor knew what she needed to do to honor her.

She stood and raised her glass. "I have an announcement. Now that I am officially the owner of this beautiful B and B, I am going to christen it with a name. Welcome to Puanani Bed and Breakfast. May all that stay here experience nothing but love."

Leilani's eyes watered as Taylor leaned over and kissed her on her cheek and said in a soft voice, "Mom is here with us. We are all together now as a family. No one will ever tear us apart again."

Leilani patted Taylor's face in silent agreement. As she sat back down, she glanced over at Jayden. By this time tomorrow, the divorce papers would be signed, and Andy and Taylor would be at the airport getting ready to board a red-eye back to the mainland. As per their agreement, the divorce would be uncontested, so the paperwork would be smooth sailing through the court. Both would walk away getting exactly what they'd come here for.

As she continued to gaze at Jayden, Taylor felt as if she was being pulled into a hypnotic trance. Everything around her became a blur as she fell deeper and deeper into Jayden's eyes. Those eyes that had always made her weak in the knees. She began to hear the sound of distant knocking in her head. There, through the dense fog of her mind, she was behind a door she swore she would never reopen. Someone or something was pounding to be let in.

Jayden? she whispered as she approached the door and reached for the knob. She could feel the vibration of the door in her hand as each knock begged to be answered. Tonight was the night she would finally open that door. Tonight was the night she would let Jayden into her heart.

Turn the knob, just turn the freakin knob. She turned the knob as the pounding grew louder. But when she opened the door, it wasn't Jayden who was standing there. *The demon.* She flinched as the figure slowly stepped out of the shadows. Her heart rate accelerated as she stared at its face before slamming the door shut and locking it. But as she backed away, she realized it wasn't the demon at all; it was herself. Or at least the part of her she'd locked away so many years ago and left to die.

The sound of Sam's voice broke Taylor free of the trance, and a blink brought her back to the moment. *What the hell?*

"Time for dessert," Sam announced as he pulled a scone the size and shape of a one-layer cake out of a box.

Jayden snorted. "Is that a—"

"Scone cake? Why, yes, it is," Sam answered. "I had my buddy make it for the special occasion."

"Let me, um, let me go get some forks, plates, and a knife to cut it." Taylor stood and bolted to the kitchen. She needed to take a breath, needed to shake out the adrenaline rush that was surging through her body, itching under her skin. She would go for a run later, her third of the day. Exhaustion was her new friend. Exhaustion numbed her emotions and blocked her from feeling. It was Taylor's go-to, it was her formula…and her formula worked. Feelings would lead to vulnerability, and vulnerability always led to the dark place in her head.

She took a breath, gathered what she came for, and headed back to the party. "You're such a freak," she mumbled to herself as she stepped out on the porch, plastered a fake smile across her face, and shook off any and all emotions begging to come out.

CHAPTER SIXTEEN

The next morning, Jayden went down to the beach at sunrise and swam out to the spot where she and Charlotte always met. Within minutes, Charlotte popped her head above the water. Jayden reached in her mesh bag and pulled out all the food at once. She was in a bit of a hurry this morning, so their usual routine of talking and lingering was sadly going to be cut short.

"I know I'm a little early today, but I need to talk to you about something. I'm um…" Tears formed in her eyes. "I'm going to be going away for a while so I won't be around. But don't you worry, Taylor and Sam are going to watch over you and make sure you get your breakfast every day." She gazed at Charlotte chomping on the lettuce. "And I want you to know that, although I won't be here, I'll be thinking about you every day, and no matter where I am, I'll close my eyes and whisper a good morning to you. If we really are connected like I think we are, then maybe the magic of the wind will carry my words to you. Think of me, and I'll think of you. And maybe that'll link us together in some way."

She pushed the last of the floating food toward Charlotte and held up her empty hands. "That's the last of it, old girl." After Charlotte took her last bite, she cocked her head. Jayden turned and floated on her back. Charlotte swam up on her chest, and although she knew it was forbidden to touch the honu, she gently stroked her shell. "I love you, sweetie. I will be thinking of you."

Charlotte stared at her for what seemed like a long time, never blinking or moving. Jayden wondered again if Charlotte understood anything she was trying to convey. Would she feel the void after Jayden left the island later this evening and feel abandoned? Charlotte was stuck in her aquatic world, and Jayden was returning to a landlocked life, both separated by forces they were not in control of. "I love you, sweet Charlotte, and I'll miss you with all my heart," she choked out.

Charlotte blinked, and with a swipe of her flipper, she turned away and slowly swam out to sea. About thirty yards out, she popped her head up and looked back, something she had never done before. Jayden raised her hand above the water and waved a final good-bye to her friend. Charlotte bobbed her head, then with a flip of her fins, disappeared.

Jayden's tears flowed down her cheeks. She stayed in the water a few extra minutes, looked toward the open ocean, and tried to memorize every inch of it. She wanted to see this view every time she closed her eyes for the rest of her life. With a heavy sigh, she finally turned and made her way back to the beach. She needed to take a shower and get ready. Taylor wanted to be at the courthouse when they opened, and no matter how much she was dreading this day, Jayden had to face it, move through it, and get on with it.

"The story of my life," she mumbled as she walked out of the water and up the beach. Why couldn't she just have one thing happen in her life that didn't end in heartache or tragedy?

It took twenty minutes to drive to the courthouse, and Jayden and Taylor sat in silence the entire way. Taylor found a parking spot close to the main entrance, and as she hopped out of the Jeep, a sharp stabbing pain shot up her leg. She stumbled. *What the hell?* She hadn't felt pain like that in months. She rubbed her thigh and couldn't help thinking there was something metaphorical about having the pain return. As though she was about to go back to where she was right after the car accident. *In more ways than one.* She sadly sighed.

Taylor held the front door for her, and once inside, they headed straight for the directory.

"This way." Taylor proceeded down a long hallway, and Jayden followed. *Is she seriously going to go through with this?* After everything they had just been through? Did any of it mean anything to her? She felt her stomach churn, and she was grateful she hadn't eaten anything yet this morning. She picked a spot on Taylor's T-shirt and hoped that if she focused on that area and didn't look around, the nausea would subside.

The office had not yet opened, so they silently sat on the bench and waited. At nine o'clock sharp, the door swung open. Taylor approached the clerk as Jayden remained seated. When she saw Taylor spread out some forms on a ledge, her body began shaking.

"Look these over," Taylor instructed as Jayden shuffled over to her.

She glanced down but didn't bother to read through them because she didn't care. "Seems pretty straightforward," she said as she reached in her purse and grabbed a pen. At this point, she just wanted to get it over with. The world around her was spinning again, and she needed to finish this up so she could sit back down. "Where am I supposed to sign?"

Taylor flipped one form over. "Here." She pointed to a line at the bottom.

Jayden took a breath and stared at the form. Her vision went in and out of focus as the dam of tears that was dangerously close to bursting began leaking. She blinked once, then twice, then squinted until she could focus on enough of the line to sign. She tightened her grip on the pen and willed her hand to move in the familiar motion of her signature.

There, she'd done it. She was now officially divorced. She took a deep breath, glanced at her signature, and laid the pen on the form. She placed her fingers around her ring. *Just treat it like a bandage.* The slower she took it off, the more it would hurt. She held her breath, and with one shift pull, the ring was off. She placed it on the form. Without saying a word or looking at Taylor, she pushed the paper, pen, and ring over to her. She needed to sit down. The walls were closing in again, and she was feeling suffocated.

❖

Taylor picked up the ring and took a moment to look at it. She moved the ring from finger to finger before she slowly slid it into her front pocket. She gently picked up the pen, let out a breath, and began to sign.

As she finished her first name and was about to begin her last, she stopped. The pesky pounding on that door inside her was beating in her head. She glanced at Jayden, then back at the form. A flood of emotions swept through her body. She, her mom, and Leilani had been robbed of so much because of Frank. How different their lives could have been. She then flashed to the mugging and all the choices she'd made as a result of that one night. She had been so desperate to create a life where no one could hurt her again that she'd failed to notice the hurt she was causing others. Especially those she loved. It was time to stop letting the pain of her past decide her future.

She put the pen down, shoved the paper in her back pocket, and grabbed Jayden's hand. "There's something I need to do first." She pulled at Jayden, who stumbled behind her.

"Taylor, what's wrong? Where are we going?"

"Just come with me." They exited the building, and she motioned for Jayden to jump in the Jeep.

As Jayden peppered her with questions, she kept her focus on the road and just repeated, "You'll see," until Jayden finally stopped asking. Twenty minutes later, they pulled down their driveway, and she ran into the house. "Sam, Leilani, Andy, come to the beach...now. It's an emergency. And bring your cameras."

She ran back outside and grabbed Jayden's hand as she hurried her to the beach.

"Taylor, you're starting to scare me, what is going on?" Jayden cried.

Sam shuffled onto the beach carrying Leilani in his arms, and Andy followed closely. Sam placed Leilani on the sand and made sure she had her balance before turning to Taylor. "What happened? What's wrong?"

"Exactly what I've been asking," Jayden said.

"Stand there." Taylor pointed to Sam. "And Leilani, scoot next to Sam. Yep, right there, and then Andy, you scoot next to Leilani."

"Taylor, what's this about?" Andy asked.

She turned to Jayden, grabbed her hands, and got down on one knee. Everyone gasped as she dug in her front pocket and pulled out Jayden's ring. "Jayden, I can't remember a time in my life when I was ever as happy as I've been this past year. Neither of us knew what we were getting into when we started this journey, and now...I'm asking you to please finish it with me."

She looked into Jayden's eyes, those beautiful crystal blue eyes of the woman she'd fallen in love with the moment she'd walked into the gym. The woman who not only completed her, but made her realize she needed to get out of her own way. It was time she opened the door to the demon of her own making. She closed her eyes and mentally kicked that goddamned hurdle out of her way once and for all. She knew she still wasn't whole, that she needed help and that it would take time. But she also knew she wanted to do it with the love of her life by her side. Together, they would conquer all of life's nightmares in some way or another.

She opened her eyes and looked at the face she wanted to wake up to every morning. "Jayden, baby, will you remarry me?"

Jayden started bouncing up and down as she said, "Yes, yes…a hundred times yes!"

Taylor stood, slid the ring on Jayden's finger, and hugged her. "I'm broken," she whispered in a soft voice, "but I'm healing."

Jayden pulled away and cupped Taylor's face. "We're all broken in one way or another. But we'll work it out. Whatever that means and whatever that looks like, we'll go through it… together."

"It might not be pretty at times. I have dark places that I hide in."

"Just promise you'll come back to me when you return to the light."

"Always." Taylor leaned in and gave her a deep, passionate kiss. When she leaned back, she said the three words that no wedding was complete without. "I love you."

❖

As they turned to walk back to the house and take the celebration inside, Jayden felt a tickle on the back of her neck. She turned around and smiled. Charlotte was bobbing in the waves, looking at her. She took a few steps toward the water as she stared for a moment, and Charlotte blinked. Maybe, just maybe, she thought, the myth about sea turtles wasn't a legend after all. Maybe Charlotte was, in her own way, a guardian of two broken souls who needed to be guided to the other. Jayden winked, and Charlotte turned and swam away.

Jayden caught up to Taylor and squeezed her hand as they walked to the house. At that moment, she knew two things: she had not only found the love of her life, she'd found a place that every part of her soul called home.

EPILOGUE

"Are you ready yet?" Taylor leaned against the master bathroom door frame.

"Baby, you know it takes me longer to get ready than you." Jayden checked herself for the umpteenth time in the mirror.

"Well, everyone's on the porch waiting."

"Well, it's not like they're going anywhere." She turned and smiled. "How do I look?" She had on a baby-blue Hawaiian sundress and a red hibiscus flower in her hair.

"Like the most beautiful wife anyone could ask for."

"Good answer." She leaned in and passionately kissed her as the butterflies took a lap around her stomach. "Ready?"

"Um, I think I'm the one whose been ready for the past twenty minutes." Taylor opened her hand palm up, and Jayden placed hers on top. A spark flew through her body as they touched, just like it had the day they'd held hands in the atrium when they were first married.

As soon as they opened the sliding glass door, Annie, her mom, Andy, Sam, and Leilani stood and applauded.

"About time," Andy said lightheartedly as he flicked a longnose lighter. He touched the flame to the waxed numeral two that was pressed into a scone cake.

Sam grabbed his ukulele and sang, "Happy anniversary to you, happy anniversary to you, happy anniversary to Jayden and Taylor, happy anniversary to you."

Jayden kissed Taylor as cheers erupted.

"Congratulations." Annie walked over to Jayden and gave her a big hug. "I'm really happy for you and Taylor."

"Thanks, Annie, and thank you for flying out. It meant a lot to Taylor."

"There isn't a thing in the world I wouldn't do for her."

"I think she feels the same about you."

"You know…" Annie leaned in. "You two really are perfect for each other."

Jayden glanced over at Taylor, who was taking a selfie with Sam. "Yeah, we are."

An hour later, after everyone had finished eating cake, she announced, "Okay, everyone, time to head to the beach."

"You go change," Taylor said to her. "I'll grab the food."

In less than five minutes, Jayden was back on the porch in her board shorts and long-sleeved surfing shirt.

Taylor was holding a wreath consisting of five heads of lettuce sewn together by celery fibers. As they led the group down to the beach, Jayden glanced over at Taylor and smiled. In the past year, Taylor had shared her story and told Jayden everything about the mugging. She knew Taylor would never totally heal from an experience like that, but that was okay. Taylor didn't have to be whole to complete Jayden. Like so many, they were both broken in their own way, and as she kept reminding Taylor, broken was the new perfect. And that was exactly what Taylor was to Jayden; she was perfect with all her dents, dings, and scratches, and Jayden wouldn't want her any other way. Perfection, she scoffed, was so overrated.

They gathered around the edge of the surf, and Taylor handed the lettuce wreath to Jayden, who promptly walked it into the ocean. It didn't take long for a head to pop up and make its way over to her.

"Hey, Charlotte, we wanted you to join in the celebration as well."

Charlotte began chomping at the wreath. The scar that disfigured a portion of her shell and back flipper caught Jayden's eye and served as a great reminder that they had all been through a lot in life.

"Thank you"—Jayden leaned in closer to Charlotte—"for being my friend." Charlotte looked up from her lettuce and bobbed her head. Jayden smiled as she softly whispered, "I always knew in my heart that you understood what I was saying."

As she left Charlotte to finish her feast and swam back to shore, she glanced at the people in her life who were huddled on the beach, laughing and talking, and in that moment, she finally understood what it felt like to be whole.

About the Author

Toni Logan grew up in the Midwest but soon transplanted to the land of lizards and saguaro cactus. She loves hanging out with friends, eating insanely delicious vegan food, traveling to the beach (any beach), and hiking in the mountains. She shares her Arizona home with a terrier mix who thinks she's a queen and four rescued cats.

Books Available from Bold Strokes Books

Busy Ain't the Half of It by Frederick Smith and Chaz Lamar Cruz. Elijah and Justin seek happily-ever-afters in LA, but are they too busy to notice happiness when it's there? (978-1-63555-944-6)

Calumet by Ali Vali. Jaxon Lavigne and Iris Long had a forbidden small-town romance that didn't last, and the consequences of that love will be uncovered fifteen years later at their high school reunion. (978-1-63555-900-2)

Her Countess to Cherish by Jane Walsh. London Society's material girl realizes there is more to life than diamonds when she falls in love with a non-binary bluestocking. (978-1-63555-902-6)

Hot Days, Heated Nights by Renee Roman. When Cole and Lee meet, instant attraction quickly flares into uncontrollable passion, but their connection might be short lived as Lee's identity is tied to her life in the city. (978-1-63555-888-3)

Never Be the Same by MA Binfield. Casey meets Olivia and sparks fly in this opposites attract romance that proves love can be found in the unlikeliest places. (978-1-63555-938-5)

Quiet Village by Eden Darry. Something not quite human is stalking Collie and her niece, and she'll be forced to work with undercover reporter Emily Lassiter if they want to get out of Hyam alive. (978-1-63555-898-2)

Shaken or Stirred by Georgia Beers. Bar owner Julia Martini and home health aide Savannah McNally attempt to weather the storms brought on by a mysterious blogger trashing the bar, family feuds they knew nothing about, and way too much advice from way too many relatives. (978-1-63555-928-6)

The Fiend in the Fog by Jess Faraday. Can four people on different trajectories work together to save the vulnerable residents of East London from the terrifying fiend in the fog before it's too late? (978-1-63555-514-1)

The Marriage Masquerade by Toni Logan. A no strings attached marriage scheme to inherit a Maui B&B uncovers unexpected attractions and a dark family secret. (978-1-63555-914-9)

Flight SQA016 by Amanda Radley. Fastidious airline passenger Olivia Lewis is used to things being a certain way. When her routine is changed by a new, attractive member of the staff, sparks fly. (978-1-63679-045-9)

Home Is Where the Heart Is by Jenny Frame. Can Archie make the countryside her home and give Ash the fairytale romance she desires? Or will the countryside and small village life all be too much for her? (978-1-63555-922-4)

Moving Forward by PJ Trebelhorn. The last person Shelby Ryan expects to be attracted to is Iris Calhoun, the sister of the man who killed her wife four years and three thousand miles ago. (978-1-63555-953-8)

Poison Pen by Jean Copeland. Debut author Kendra Blake is finally living her best life until a nasty book review and exposed secrets threaten her promising new romance with aspiring journalist Alison Chatterley. (978-1-63555-849-4)

Seasons for Change by KC Richardson. Love, laughter, and trust develop for Shawn and Morgan throughout the changing seasons of Lake Tahoe. (978-1-63555-882-1)

Summer Lovin' by Julie Cannon. Three different women, three exotic locations, one unforgettable summer. What do you think will happen? (978-1-63555-920-0)

Unbridled by D. Jackson Leigh. A visit to a local stable turns into more than riding lessons between a novel writer and an equestrian with a taste for power play. (978-1-63555-847-0)

VIP by Jackie D. In a town where relationships are forged and shattered by perception, sometimes even love can't change who you really are. (978-1-63555-908-8)

Yearning by Gun Brooke. The sleepy town of Dennamore has an irresistible pull on those who've moved away. The mystery Darian Benson and Samantha Pike uncover will change them forever, but the love they find along the way just might be the key to saving themselves. (978-1-63555-757-2)

A Turn of Fate by Ronica Black. Will Nev and Kinsley finally face their painful past and relent to their powerful, forbidden attraction? Or will facing their past be too much to fight through? (978-1-63555-930-9)

Desires After Dark by MJ Williamz. When her human lover falls deathly ill, Alex, a vampire, must decide which is worse, letting her go or condemning her to everlasting life. (978-1-63555-940-8)

Her Consigliere by Carsen Taite. FBI agent Royal Scott swore an oath to uphold the law, and criminal defense attorney Siobhan Collins pledged her loyalty to the only family she's ever known, but will their love be stronger than the bonds they've vowed to others, or will their competing allegiances tear them apart? (978-1-63555-924-8)

In Our Words: Queer Stories from Black, Indigenous, and People of Color Writers. Stories selected by Anne Shade and Edited by Victoria Villaseñor. Comprising both the renowned and emerging voices of Black, Indigenous, and People of Color authors, this thoughtfully curated collection of short stories explores the intersection of racial and queer identity. (978-1-63555-936-1)

Measure of Devotion by CF Frizzell. Disguised as her late twin brother, Catherine Samson enters the Civil War to defend the Constitution as a Union soldier, never expecting her life to be altered by a Gettysburg farmer's daughter. (978-1-63555-951-4)

Not Guilty by Brit Ryder. Claire Weaver and Emery Pearson's day jobs clash, even as their desire for each other burns, and a discreet sex-only arrangement is the only option. (978-1-63555-896-8)

Opposites Attract: Butch/Femme Romances by Meghan O'Brien, Aurora Rey, Angie Williams. Sometimes opposites really do attract. Fall in love with these butch/femme romance novellas. (978-1-63555-784-8)

Swift Vengeance by Jean Copeland, Jackie D, Erin Zak. A journalist becomes the subject of her own investigation when sudden strange, violent visions summon her to a summer retreat and into the arms of a killer's possible next victim. (978-1-63555-880-7)

Under Her Influence by Amanda Radley. On their path to #truelove, will Beth and Jemma discover that reality is even better than illusion? (978-1-63555-963-7)

Wasteland by Kristin Keppler & Allisa Bahney. Danielle Clark is fighting against the National Armed Forces and finds peace as a scavenger, until the NAF general's daughter, Katelyn Turner, shows up on her doorstep and brings the fight right back to her. (978-1-63555-935-4)

When in Doubt by VK Powell. Police officer Jeri Wylder thinks she committed a crime in the line of duty but can't remember, until details emerge pointing to a cover-up by those close to her. (978-1-63555-955-2)

A Woman to Treasure by Ali Vali. An ancient scroll isn't the only treasure Levi Montbard finds as she starts her hunt for the truth—all she has to do is prove to Yasmine Hassani that there's more to her than an adventurous soul. (978-1-63555-890-6)

Before. After. Always. by Morgan Lee Miller. Still reeling from her tragic past, Eliza Walsh has sworn off taking risks, until Blake Navarro turns her world right-side up, making her question if falling in love again is worth it. (978-1-63555-845-6)

Bet the Farm by Fiona Riley. Lauren Calloway's luxury real estate sale of the century comes to a screeching halt when dairy farm heiress, and one-night stand, Thea Boudreaux calls her bluff. (978-1-63555-731-2)

Cowgirl by Nance Sparks. The last thing Aren expects is to fall for Carol. Sharing her home is one thing, but sharing her heart means sharing the demons in her past and risking everything to keep Carol safe. (978-1-63555-877-7)

Give In to Me by Elle Spencer. Gabriela Talbot never expected to sleep with her favorite author—certainly not after the scathing review she'd given Whitney Ainsworth's latest book. (978-1-63555-910-1)

Hidden Dreams by Shelley Thrasher. A lethal virus and its resulting vision send Texan Barbara Allan and her lovely guide, Dara, on a journey up Cambodia's Mekong River in search of Barbara's mother's mystifying past. (978-1-63555-856-2)

In the Spotlight by Lesley Davis. For actresses Cole Calder and Eris Whyte, their chance at love runs out fast when a fan's adoration turns to obsession. (978-1-63555-926-2)

Origins by Jen Jensen. Jamis Bachman is pulled into a dangerous mystery that becomes personal when she learns the truth of her origins as a ghost hunter. (978-1-63555-837-1)

Pursuit: A Victorian Entertainment by Felice Picano. An intelligent, handsome, ruthlessly ambitious young man who rose from the slums to become the right-hand man of the Lord Exchequer of England will stop at nothing as he pursues his Lord's vanished wife across Continental Europe. (978-1-63555-870-8)

Unrivaled by Radclyffe. Zoey Cohen will never accept second place in matters of the heart, even when her rival is a career, and Declan Black has nothing left to give of herself or her heart. (978-1-63679-013-8)

A Fae Tale by Genevieve McCluer. Dovana comes to terms with her changing feelings for her lifelong best friend and fae, Roze. (978-1-63555-918-7)

Accidental Desperados by Lee Lynch. Life is clobbering Berry, Jaudon, and their long romance. The arrival of directionless baby dyke MJ doesn't help. Can they find their passion again—and keep it? (978 1 63555 182 3)

Always Believe by Aimée. Greyson Walsden is pursuing ordination as an Anglican priest. Angela Arlingham doesn't believe in God. Do they follow their vocation or their hearts? (978-1-63555-912-5)

Best of the Wrong Reasons by Sander Santiago. For Fin Ness and Orion Starr, it takes a funeral to remind them that love is worth living for. (978-1-63555-867-8)

Courage by Jesse J. Thoma. No matter how often Natasha Parsons and Tommy Finch clash on the job, an undeniable attraction simmers just beneath the surface. Can they find the courage to change so love has room to grow? (978-1-63555-802-9)

I Am Chris by R Kent. There's one saving grace to losing everything and moving away. Nobody knows her as Chrissy Taylor. Now Chris can live who he truly is. (978-1-63555-904-0)

The Princess and the Odium by Sam Ledel. Jastyn and Princess Aurelia return to Venostes and join their families in a battle against the dark force to take back their homeland for a chance at a better tomorrow. (978-1-63555-894-4)

The Queen Has a Cold by Jane Kolven. What happens when the heir to the throne isn't a prince or a princess? (978-1-63555-878-4)

The Secret Poet by Georgia Beers. Agreeing to help her brother woo Zoe Blake seemed like a good idea to Morgan Thompson at first…until she realizes she's actually wooing Zoe for herself… (978-1-63555-858-6)

You Again by Aurora Rey. For high school sweethearts Kate Cormier and Sutton Guidry, the second chance might be the only one that matters. (978-1-63555-791-6)